About the Authors

Frank Dirscherl is the author of many novels, including the Amazon bestselling *The Wraith* and *Sanderson of Metro*, as well as several short stories. His T*he Wraith Dread Avenger of the Underworld* books have been enjoyed by readers all over the world.

A librarian with over thirty years experience, Frank has also worked at a book wholesaler, a specialist medical practice and as a tutor in the writing and producing of comic books. His interests include reading, traveling, history, politics, architecture and the environment.

Frank lives in the Illawarra on the south coast of New South Wales, Australia, with his wife and daughter, and is always working on his latest literary endeavors.

Stephen J. Semones, filmmaker and founder of Sir Reel Films, began writing at an early age to satisfy his need to tell stories. Since then, he has gone on to develop some of the most ambitious projects in independent film, including the short film, *The Wraith: Eyes of Judgment*, and the web-series, *Nothing's at Stake*. Semi-retired from film, Stephen is focusing on writing fiction and online film reviews and interviews. Now residing in the beautiful Appalachian Mountains in Southwest Virginia, Stephen lives with his wife, Faith, and today works mainly as a pastor.

GLOWING EYES MEDIA

Praise for *Sanderson of Metro*
Amazon bestseller

"Once shrouded in mystery, The Wraith's stunning origin is finally revealed. Dirscherl and Nash have written one hell of an adventure novel filled with myth, intrigue, and excitement. Highly recommended reading."

- A.P. Fuchs, writer, *The Axiom-man Saga, The Way of the Fog, Undead World trilogy*

"Recommended for Wraith and pulp hero fans."

– Leon Mallett, *Amazon*

"At the end of the day, this novel is a worthy addition to The Wraith's continuing story and a necessary purchase if you're a fan of the character. It's also just a flat out enjoyable reading experience."

– Marcus Bucklin, *Amazon*

"The story is well written, and the Paul Sanderson character fleshed out fairly well...I highly recommend this well written entry for all comic book fans."

– Virginia E. Johnson, *Amazon*

Praise for *Valley of Evil*

"The second Wraith novel is an improvement, I think. Right from the start Dirscherl throws you into the middle of crazy action.... This book is a whole lot of superheroic pulp fun, and the good news is there seems to be more to come...I look forward to some more of the same."

– Richard Scott, *Super Reader* website

"I think (Dirscherl) really captured a noir element with (his) voice."

– Joshua Gamon, writer, *Abigail & Rox, Digital Webbing Presents*

"I did quite enjoy the books. Best of all, it wasn't overly sex-filled or gory—I can't stand most modern superhero comics that show such things or have the heroes just swear and swear. So *The Wraith* (and *Valley of Evil*) was just up my alley."

– Greg Gick, writer, *The Werewolf of Rutherford Grange, Tales of the Shadowmen, Secret Agent X Vol. 2*

"The Dread Avenger is back. After battling the Cobra in his first prose adventure, The Wraith returns to face all new challenges from Metro City's greatest villains, most notably Hong Kong drug kingpin Ma Tzi. As with his first Wraith novel, Frank Dirscherl treats us to a pulp-inspired adventure that keeps readers on the edge of their seat. You have to read this novel in one sitting."

– Bobby Nash, writer, *Evil Ways, Fantastix, Lance Star*

"In the past five years there has been a tremendous resurgence in pulp fiction centering on the old heroic pulps. Young writers have started taking up the mantle of old masters like Walter Gibson and Lester Dent and begun creating their own avengers in tales of genuine purple prose. Among the best of this new generation of wordsmiths is Australian, Frank Dirscherl and the exploits of his modern pulp paladin, The Wraith. This is grand pulp!"

– Ron Fortier, writer, *The Spider, Brother Bones, Domino Lady*

Praise for *Crossfire*

"Stephen did a fantastic job of bringing Frank Dirscherl's character to life!"
- Adam DiTroia, composer, *The Wraith: Eyes of Judgment*, MTV, Fox Sports

"Loved the book!! Can't wait for the next installment..."
- Larry Mainland, actor, *The Walking Dead, Lawless, The Three Stooges*

"The action comes swift, and doesn't stop until the final pages. *Crossfire* tells a great story of betrayal and revenge."
- C.R. Blevins, writer, *A Western Tale*

"This was my first introduction to The Wraith and I was not disappointed. The action comes swift, and doesn't stop until the final pages.... If you love a good action/hero story, you will certainly enjoy reading *Crossfire*."
- Ally, *Amazon*

"Makes me want more...should be the next series on Netflix..."
- Bill Lancaster, *Amazon*

"Another excellent entry in The Wraith Adventures series. Thoroughly recommended for Wraith fans and fans of pulp super-heroics."
- Leon Mallett, *Amazon*

Praise for *Cult of the Damned*

"Only by the first three pages, Frank Dirscherl wonderfully captures a dark and mysterious atmosphere, one that leaves the reader with a cryptic and eerie sensation; one that makes me cold just thinking about it."

> – Rennie Cowan, writer/director, *The Thriller Idol: A Tribute to the Legacy of Michael Jackson, Kade the Conqueror*

"Frank Dirscherl pulls you into the world of The Wraith from the first sentence and refuses to let you go until the last one."

> – Stephen J. Semones, writer/director, *Beyond the Lens, Crossfire, The Wraith: Eyes of Judgment*

"The Wraith is one of my favorite characters and every time Frank Dirscherl puts pen to paper I know I'm in for a real treat."

> – A.P. Fuchs, writer, *The Axiom-man Saga, The Way of the Fog, Undead World trilogy*

Praise for *Cry of the Werewolf*

"Frank Dirscherl delivers beyond measure.... The solid characters, settings and story really propel you page to page and leave you hanging on for more."
- Stephen J. Semones, writer/director, *Beyond the Lens, Crossfire, The Wraith: Eyes of Judgment*

"Each new installment in *The Wraith Adventures* series is a guaranteed good time filled with high adventure, romance and pulpy fun. Dirscherl is at the top of his form."
- A.P. Fuchs, writer, *The Axiom-man Saga, The Way of the Fog, Undead World trilogy*

"The writing is well done and well edited, and is filled with that distinct Dirscherl style of pulp that I enjoy so much. The book is a perfect example of what Neo Pulp/Superhero and Horror fiction can be and is a worthy addition to any fan's collection."
- Marcus Bucklin, *Amazon*

Praise for *Vendetta*

"...in all a great brew that had me hooked for the whole ride. Now bring on the next book, Frank..."

– Leon Mallett, *Amazon*

"This book starts with a literal bang and doesn't let the foot off of the gas until the very last page. The book is well plotted and moves at a breakneck pace, making it an enjoyable, short read. I loved this book very much as a fan of The Wraith and I believe that anyone who is a fan of the series should consider this required reading."

– Marcus Bucklin, *Amazon*

Praise for *Zombies Attack!* in *Metahumans vs the Undead*

"This compilation of superheroes vs evil offers top entertainment for superhero lovers! Frank Dirscherl and others are at their best with their contributed stories. I will now pursue other stories written by these authors, such as those involving Mr. Dirscherl's The Wraith. This type of reading enjoyment knows no end!"

–   Ramona Wingart, writer, *Where is Brother Beaver?*, *Emily Suzanne Smith!*

Praise for *Werewolves Attack!* in *Metahumans vs Werewolves*

"Always a great read. Can never put it down once you get started... "

– Geraldine L. Lewis, *Amazon*

BY STEPHEN J. SEMONES

FICTION

Crossfire (with Frank Dirscherl)
Gloom
Gloom: Fog of War
Gloom: Gloom's Day
Gloom: Sic Sempter Tyrannis
The Sacrifice of Candace Blake
Unhinged
The Killing Tree

NON-FICTION

*The Wraith: Eyes of Judgment – The Official Script Book
& Movie Guide* (with Frank Dirscherl)
Beyond the Lens

BY FRANK DIRSCHERL

FICTION

The Wraith Dread Avenger of the Underworld series

Sanderson of Metro (with Bobby Nash)
Serpent Rising (with Greg Gick)
The Wraith
Valley of Evil
Crossfire (with Stephen J. Semones)
Cult of the Damned
Cry of the Werewolf
Swamp Witch of Satan's Forest (with Ray MacKay)
Vendetta
Lady Wraith (with Adam Oravec) - COMING SOON

SHORT STORY COLLECTIONS

Metahumans vs. the Undead
Metahumans vs. Werewolves
Metahumans vs. Robots
Metahumans vs. the Ultimate Evil
Lance Star – Sky Ranger Vol. 1

NON-FICTION

The Wraith: Eyes of Judgment – The Official Script Book & Movie Guide
(with Stephen J. Semones)
The Hitchers of Oz
Beyond the Lens (edited)

www.glowingeyesmedia.com

CROSSFIRE

The Wraith Dread Avenger of the Underworld #3

by

Frank Dirscherl &
Stephen J. Semones

GLOWING EYES MEDIA
WOLLONGONG

GLOWING EYES MEDIA
PO Box 31
Wollongong NSW 2520

ISBN 978-0-6457475-2-2

PUBLISHED BY GLOWING EYES MEDIA, January 2025
www.glowingeyesmedia.com
FRONT COVER ART by Brian & Marie Bridgeforth of Bridgeforth Design Studio
INTERIOR DESIGN by Frank Dirscherl
EDITED by Frank Dirscherl and Joanne Lane at FirstEditing.com
FIRST PUBLISHED IN 2012
SECOND EDITION

For more on *Crossfire*
visit www.glowingeyesmedia.com

Text set in Garamond-Normal. Printed and bound in the USA

NATIONAL LIBRARY OF AUSTRALIA

A catalogue record for this book is available from the National Library of Australia

So far...but the story goes on...

For my family and my fans - FD

For Frank:

An amazing friend...this is all for you - SS

CROSSFIRE

~ Prologue ~

The helicopter drowned out almost every other sound. Jackson Thomas sat across from his three fellow soldiers and looked at them proudly. They were ready for anything and he assumed this would be another routine mission for them all. Lighting his trademark Cuban cigar, he took the smoke gently in, savored it briefly, and exhaled two streams of thick smoke out his nose. He loved this part of a mission: the calm before the storm. They had been called Devil Company when they were all marines, and even now, as private mercenaries, nothing had changed - they still lived up to their name.

Thomas had once been a captain in the United States Marine Corps. He was a hard-hitting, take-no-prisoners officer that had a reputation for being less than cordial. After several run-ins with authority, he decided to go where the money was and started his own private mercenary regiment. His reputation far preceded him and because most people chose not to cross him he had earned the nickname

Crossfire. His tattoo of black crosshairs on the left side of his neck demonstrated his high tolerance for pain. He seemed to welcome it, but even worse, he seemed to enjoy inflicting it upon others. No one wanted to get in his bad books, nor in the middle of a problem he was mixed up in, so most soldiers avoided him wherever possible.

He was a very intimidating man who, standing a hair over six feet tall, could look you directly in the eye and make you feel very uneasy. His angular and chiseled face made his expression seem angry or displeased. The intimidation factor was enhanced by his muscular physique. Most officers avoided him while lower rank soldiers feared the very sight of him.

There were very few men who could stand eye to eye with Crossfire and not feel as if they were about to die at his hand. He spoke very little and he would stare people down with a deep intensity radiating from his dark brown eyes.

Before he finally retired from the marines as a captain, he had decided to search for what he considered the *baddest of the bad*. After hunting for what felt an eternity, he put together Devil Company and tested them out with black-ops missions while they were still all enlisted marines. Recruiting from within made complete sense to him and, over time, Crossfire formed his squad of mercenaries. They were a force to be reckoned with as marines and now that they only answered to him, they were even deadlier than before.

The first to be recruited into Devil Company was Staff Sergeant Randy "Dog" Ennis. He had earned the name *Dog* in basic training as a marine. The first day of basic, his drill sergeant got in his face, as they were want to do, and screamed at Randy to do over a hundred sit-ups. Randy, in revenge, decided to stop brushing his teeth so that when his drill sergeant got in his face again he would smell his horrid breath and leave him alone. His plan didn't work, but it helped earn him his nickname, as his breath smelled just like a dog's.

Randy was a short, stout man who was strong and had a personality that bordered on madness thanks to some extreme behavior. Randy had forced his superior to promote him by holding a knife to his neck. Much later a commanding officer recommended Randy for court marshal and was later found dead in his office with a knife in his chest. Fortunately Randy had an iron-clad alibi and was soon released back on duty.

Word of Randy reached Crossfire, who proceeded to scout him out for his squad. As he dug deeper into his past, he found Randy was essentially a criminal wearing a marine's uniform. Randy's file was thicker than most books Crossfire had read. From grand theft auto to burglary and larceny, Randy Ennis joined the marines to escape judicial persecution. Thinking he had no other option, Randy put his skills to use for the U.S. government. His violent temper, lack of conscience, and overall lust for blood showed Crossfire he was a must-have for Devil Company.

The second to join the company came by recommendation of Randy Ennis. Carlos "Mexico" Alverez had been in basic training with Randy and they soon became close friends. It was suspected that Alverez had a hand in killing the commanding officer responsible for Randy's court marshal, but no one had the fortitude, or evidence, to come forward and make any charges stick. Carlos' quick Latino temper fit in well with Randy's lust for blood, and they became inseparable friends. Like a pack of wild dogs, if someone had an issue with one man, they instantly had one with the other. They both, even as basic training recruits, earned a reputation for violence and they loved it.

Despite only standing five foot nine, Alverez was no small man. He had been in and out of Mexican jails and institutions since he was thirteen years old and was in top shape. At first glance, many thought he was a professional athlete until they got a closer look at him, and saw the dissipation apparent in his face. For Alvarez most days were spent fighting with other inmates or lifting weights, so his strength was almost inhuman compared to a normal man. His darkened complexion and hair give him an exotic look, but his multiple tattoos said otherwise. With Mexican heritage body art covering his arms, chest, and neck, his appearance was intimidating.

When Crossfire asked him to fight another soldier in hand to hand combat in order to prove himself for Devil Company, Carlos immediately snapped the soldier's neck, killing him before he even had a chance. It was the quickest fight Crossfire had ever seen and he immediately welcomed Alverez into Devil Company with open arms.

The last man to enter the squad was Frank "Zero" Piper. Frank came from a long line of marines and was a proud man the day he joined the corps. At seventeen his dad gave him the option of joining the marines or being disowned by his family, so he chose basic training almost without hesitation. Growing up, he felt as if he had a higher calling than the marines, but ultimately knew his career would lie in the corps.

Training hard his last year of high school, Frank took a lot of abuse from fellow students. They would tease him and called him *G.I. Joe* or *Captain America* for his dedication to becoming a soldier. Frank would fight back and he was almost expelled from school numerous times as a result. His father had bred a marine corps machine in his son and was proud the day he left for basic training.

Upon entering boot camp, Frank soon found out that it wasn't what he'd expected. With his gung-ho attitude concerning his love of being a soldier, he found himself the target of even more daily ridicule from his fellow marines. Wondering how soldiers who defend their country could chastise another for patriotism, Frank questioned whether or not he had made the right choice with his military career.

One day, while running through the obstacle course, a few marines decided to have a little fun when Frank took to the rope bridge. The bridge was only about ten feet high and nearly twice as long. When Frank made the halfway mark, two of them began to shake the bridge so he slipped and almost fell off. In that moment, as he struggled to hang on and the other marines roared with laughter below him, something inside him snapped. When he reached the other side he single-handedly took down the two marines who had started the incident. He grabbed one by the throat and he gouged the other's eyes, injuring them enough to send them to sick bay for a week.

The incident caught Crossfire's eye and he made sure, through his connections, that Frank Piper be granted a reduced punishment. Frank was grateful to Crossfire and eagerly joined him in Devil Company.

Standing six foot four, Frank was the tallest and leanest soldier in the company, which made for some good-natured ribbing. A bean pole they called him. However, when his skills on the firing range were put to the test for his Devil Company recruitment, he failed miserably and missed every single target. He earned the nickname Zero on the spot. After failing target practice, he stood up to Crossfire and told him to give him another shot. Crossfire admired his dedication and gave him the second chance he yearned for.

For the next test, he had Frank take up position on top of a building outside the command post on the marine base. His orders were to shoot the hat off the next officer to walk out of the building. Without hesitation, Frank fired at the first officer he saw, blew the hat clean off their head, and that night was celebrated as the official sniper of Devil Company. He may have been horrible at close range firing, but his long range ability was phenomenal. Crossfire saw something in Frank that he warmed to and brought him onboard. Frank never lived down the nickname Zero, but was still accepted as a brother within Devil Company.

Crossfire later explained to the officer that it was a ricochet from the nearby shooting range. Despite feeling angry, the officer bought the story and never realized how close he had been to death.

~ Chapter 1 ~

IRAQ BORDER - DECEMBER 22 1990

As the helicopter touched down, the dust and loose earth swirled around the desert in a giant circular motion. Even though it was after midnight, the heat could still be seen shimmering in the moonlight. As soon as the chopper touched down, Crossfire hopped from the passenger hold into the night air. He felt the earth crunch under his heavy boots as he hit the ground. Eyeing his surroundings, he flipped his cigar away and motioned for the pilot to kill the engines. With a low swooping sound, the blades slowed to a stop.

Dressed in pitch-black clothing, Crossfire seemed to blend into the darkness and his men always had a hard time seeing him without their night-vision goggles. He raised his arm outward in an L-shape and the squad jumped from the helicopter. Without saying a word, he threw his arm forward and, knowing their roles in the squad, they broke off and silently crept past him. Zero screwed the suppressor to the front of his fifty caliber sniper rifle and moved to a small embankment in the front. Giving a nod back to his squad, Dog and Mexico moved off to his right and left respectively. Crossfire headed up the middle as he made his way slowly to the small embankment.

They were just three clicks away from their target: the small village of Karbah. Sitting just across the Iraq border, Karbah was also close to Saudi Arabia and Kuwait. It was predominantly a farming village and its people were fervently against their dictator Saddam Hussein and his regime, though they did nothing to fuel any discontent for fear of savage reprisal. It wasn't uncommon for Iraqi soldiers to frequent Karbah on their way to patrol the border and take whatever they wanted for food or fuel.

Crossfire saw the lights of Karbah on the distant horizon. Looking down at Zero, he sought confirmation that it was safe to enter the target village from his soldier and grinned when Zero nodded in agreement. They had roughly a thirty minute walk before they reached their destination and something told Crossfire deep inside to be wary. He always trusted his gut and never second-guessed his intuition. Staring at the town, he reached up and gently touched the microphone transmitter attached to his cap.

"Be alert. Something tells me to keep our eyes open for surprises. Move out."

Without hesitation, Devil Company made their way down the embankment and into the valley below. Moving like ghosts through the night, they slowly and methodically made their way toward the village.

* * * * * *

When they were two hundred yards from the village outskirts, Zero broke off and set his rifle up beside three very large boulders. Quickly unpacking the rifle tripod, he dropped and dug himself into his post. He flipped the cap off of his scope, closed one eye and realized a complete view of the small village. He gave the thumbs-up to Crossfire and the squad continued moving toward Karbah.

From his position, Zero could see Crossfire, with Mexico on his left, motion for him to move ahead and circle his side of the village. With an acknowledging nod, Mexico cocked his M16 sub-machine gun and disappeared into the darkness as he quickly followed orders. Crossfire then motioned for Dog to take point and move ahead into the village. Dog gave an understanding nod as he cocked his M60 machine gun and slowly crept up the main road leading into the village. Crossfire circled out to the right, cocked his M16, and raised it into an offensive stance.

"Sir, I have all three of you in sight. No activity can be seen from my vantage point. You're all clear to enter," Zero said as he watched them through his sniper scope. He kept his finger on the trigger in case he had to assist in a split second.

* * * * * *

Mexico was the first to enter Karbah. The village was spread out with small farm huts and stone houses scattered randomly for several hundred yards. He could see nothing out of the ordinary. Reaching up, he clicked the transmitter on his hat.

"Clear on my side. Over," Mexico said as he passed by a small house. He eyed his surroundings as he secured the area.

* * * * * *

Dog entered the village next, moving stealthily up the street. He knelt beside a small barn noting camels inside eating. Securing his position, he clicked his transmitter and confirmed his status.

"Clear down the middle. Over," Dog said, eyeing the barn curiously.

* * * * * *

"It looks like everyone is asleep, sir. You're clear to enter," Zero said over the radio.

As Crossfire stepped around a small house, he suddenly had a strange feeling wash over him. It was as if fear had struck him right to his core, a feeling he was not familiar with. Raising his machinegun to his chin, he quickly glanced around in every direction. He made contact with both Mexico and Dog and gave them each an acknowledging nod to proceed through the village. Turning back to look toward the opposite end of town where the team had came from, he saw something. A truck. It slowly lumbered toward them.

It looked almost military in origin, with green paint and a rag top covering the cargo, but the door reading *LATHAM INDUSTRIES* made Crossfire feel uneasy. He knew that a private American company had no business in the middle of a war, which made him question the company's allegiance.

The wooden crates in the truck bed were all stamped with the same company name and he couldn't help but wonder why the truck was here. Then it hit him hard. This private company was after the same thing he was hired to find.

Crossfire didn't know much about his mission other than he was supposed to retrieve some relic that was supposedly being kept by the people of Karbah. The U.S. government could only speculate it was here and the actual existence of the relic could be little more than a myth, so they had hired Devil Company to investigate first before committing troops. If they were caught, the government could deny all knowledge of their actions and claim they were some rogue group hired by an unknown party. Crossfire knew his country would turn its back on them if they failed and were captured, so in his mind, that wasn't an option.

The relic was rumored to be an ancient coin with some sort of religious significance and power, the likes of which he didn't know, nor did he really care. His mission was to get this coin before anyone else could. That was all he knew, but staring at the truck now, he knew at least one other person had the same intention.

As they eased toward the slowly moving truck, the three mercenaries of Devil Company crept slowly through the shadows in complete silence, then stopped and watched the truck with weapons at the ready. The truck proceeded slowly down the main street before parking in an alcove near the edge of town. Two men exited the vehicle and disappeared into the adjacent building, a somewhat larger hut than those surrounding it.

Making their way toward the truck, Crossfire signaled for Dog to check out the cargo while he and Mexico held his cover. Dog shone a small light into the truck bed and examined the cargo carefully.

"All wooden crates, sir," Dog whispered, "and all are labeled Latham Industries."

Naturally unsure of their contents, he threw Crossfire a puzzled look. Mexico and Crossfire looked at each other and then eyed their surroundings. Something just wasn't right and Crossfire knew they all felt it now. He flipped the transmitter microphone on his hat and cautiously backed away from the truck.

"Zero, I need an eye on the north end," Crossfire said uneasily.

Zero didn't respond.

"Zero! I need an eye on the north end. Do you copy?"

Again, nothing.

Eyeing the other two members of Devil Company, Crossfire shook his head and motioned for them to fall back. As they each retraced their steps, gunshots rang out across the town from every direction. Now separated, they were all sitting targets for an ambush.

"Get down and dig in! We're under fire!" Crossfire yelled over his transmitter.

Crouching down and pinning his back against a small stone house, Crossfire tried to look in the direction of the gunfire. Bullets ripped up the earth beside him and bounced off of the house. He dropped to the ground, crawled to the door, and kicked it with his boot. The door splintered open and he rolled inside. As he closed the door behind him, bullets riddled the house and kicked up dirt and debris all around him. Still on the ground, he looked around and noted the house was empty apart from the same wooden crates in the truck. He crawled underneath a window and peered outside as best he could.

He saw that Mexico was badly wounded and bleeding profusely from his stomach and side. He was hunched against a house across the small road and sitting between two compact, stone walls. He had one arm across his waist holding his wound while he tried to change his magazine with the other. It looked bleak for Mexico, but Crossfire knew his men wouldn't go down without wiping their enemies from the map. He couldn't see Dog, but heard the return gunfire nearby and assumed he was still in good shape.

Crossfire realized the overlapping fields of fire had pinned them down in separate positions and they'd walked into a set-up. Devil Company was completely boxed in and he knew the only way they would escape was to shoot their way out. His years of training had prepared him for situations such as this, but he knew it wasn't going to end well for someone, he just hoped it wasn't Devil Company.

"Dog! We're boxed in and cut off. They have us surrounded. Mexico is down from what I can tell. We're going to have to blow our way out and try to make it to that truck," Crossfire said loudly over the gunfire into his transmitter. He looked out the window again and saw Mexico trying to sit up to return fire. Bullets blew dirt up all around him and he sat back down between the two walls.

"I've got a visual, Mexico is hit badly. I'm covering his six so he can try and make it to you," Dog screamed back.

"Negative, Dog. We're all pinned down. We'll have to blow our way out. You know what to do. Let me know when you're ready for the smoke."

"Copy that, sir! Give me sixty seconds and then pop the smoke. I'll get Mexico and rendezvous with you at the truck. Over," Dog yelled.

Crossfire looked at his watch. He knew what Dog was capable of and only hoped that it would be enough of a diversion to cover them so they could make it to the truck.

There was no exit the way they had come. He pulled a smoke grenade from his hip and set it beside him at the ready. Checking his watch again, he only had twenty seconds left and he knew he had to be ready to move.

He peered out the window again and saw Mexico hunched over between the two walls. He was barely moving and Crossfire knew he had only minutes to live. The pool of blood around Mexico was slowly spreading to the narrow road between them. His front was saturated and Crossfire knew that whoever shot him had either been extremely lucky or knew how to aim for major organs and arteries.

He looked at his watch once again and saw he had five seconds left. He counted them down in his head and pulled the pin on the smoke grenade. He tossed it out the window above his head and tried to aim it away from Mexico. A loud pop and then hiss was heard over the gunshots. Crossfire counted to five and looked out the window again. Smoke was billowing into the air from the small grenade, partially obstructing his friend from view.

"Move out!" Crossfire screamed into the transmitter as he burst through the door of the house. As soon as the outside air hit his face, bullets whizzed into the ground and house all around him. Gunfire continued in the distance and he knew that Dog had to be laying down random cover fire to confuse their assailants so he could make it to Mexico through the smoke. With the truck within reach, Crossfire turned and fired randomly around the ridge overlooking Karbah.

Smoke filled the air and made it hard to see anything. His smoke grenade had landed in the ideal place to dissipate evenly across town and given them the best cover to make it to the truck. The truck was locked, so without hesitation, Crossfire elbowed the glass and shattered the passenger side window. Reaching in, he unlocked the door, opened it, and jumped inside. He crawled across the bench seat to the driver side and looked for keys. Nothing. Dropping down to the floor, he immediately pulled the steering column loose and began stripping the wires.

* * * * * *

Dog, struggling to keep Mexico on his feet with his left arm, fired shots randomly around with his right. Drifting in and out of consciousness, Mexico was struggling to stay upright.

"Come on brother. Just a few more feet and we're home free. Don't let go!" Dog screamed at Mexico as they scrambled toward the truck.

He continued to pull Mexico along as he fired off shots in every direction in hope of distracting the shooters in the smoke. With the truck just ahead, Dog knew it was time. Dropping his M16 and letting it dangle from the strap around his shoulder, he pulled a small metal box from his bandolier.

As the demolitions expert in Devil Company, Dog had to set charges within seconds. That's exactly what he had done just before Crossfire threw the smoke grenade. With bullets hitting within inches of him, Dog had thrown several C4 charges through the windows of nearby homes and barns. He lost count of how many he'd thrown, but with the truck so close, he knew it was time to put his plan into motion, to create the secondary diversion. Flicking the remote switch on the small metal box, Dog winced and tightened his body as he prepared for what was about to happen.

* * * * * *

As Crossfire twisted the final two wires together and the truck engine fired up, a deafening roar shook the earth. He knew it had to be Dog. The smoke was merely a tactic to regroup, but this diversion was just what they needed for escape. The massive explosion bounced the truck so hard that he felt as if it was going to turn on its side. He sat up and glanced into the side-view mirror and smiled as he realized just how deadly his squad was. Fire and black smoke rose into the sky from several places in giant pillars.

Crossfire didn't know how many charges Dog had thrown, but judging by the carnage and devastation there must have been a few. He could faintly see chunks of rock and debris falling around him. He figured Dog had virtually leveled Karbah with the flick of a switch.

The door opened beside him and without hesitation, Crossfire readied his weapon and almost fired. Dog shoved Mexico in and climbed in behind him. He smiled at Crossfire as he lowered his weapon.

"Easy there sir," Dog said as he closed the door behind him.

The gunfire started again and they could see dirt burst into little clouds all around the truck.

"Why aren't they shooting the truck, sir?" Dog questioned as Crossfire revved up the engine and threw the truck into first gear.

"The cargo. Look behind us," Crossfire returned.

Dog turned to look behind them and saw one of the crates had been slightly opened from the explosion. Gold objects and artifacts spilled all over the truck bed from the crate.

"I don't get it," Dog said.

"It's valuable and they don't want to risk damaging it."

"It's just gold, sir."

"Obviously it's not just gold, Dog. Hang on," Crossfire said as he changed gears and whipped the truck around back in the direction they had come.

"What are you doing sir?" Dog questioned.

"Taking us home," Crossfire said and shot him an angry look that said one should never question a superior. The look was a warning to Dog to keep his mouth shut and not question his motives. Taking the hint, Dog leaned out of the broken window with his gun and fired toward the ridge.

The truck bounced through what was left of the village at breakneck speed. They could feel the heat on their faces as they tore through the blazing infernos on either side of them. Exiting the same way they had originally come in, Crossfire directed the truck toward Zero's position. He hadn't heard from him for some time and hadn't had time to check on his status. He had to know what happened to him.

He whipped the truck to a stop by the large boulders where they had last seen Zero. They also gave him enough cover to get out and check around. Exiting the truck he saw immediately it wasn't good news. Zero was lying motionless in the dirt.

Checking him and turning him over, he could see Zero had been shot in the back of the head, execution style. He undoubtedly never heard his assassin coming. He had died covering his squad and Crossfire would never forget his sacrifice. With a mix of anger and sadness, Crossfire hoisted Zero's body onto his shoulder and shoved the corpse into the truck beside Mexico. Getting back inside, he heard a single gunshot and instantly saw Dog slump forward hitting his head on the windshield. Blood gushed from the side of his head and Crossfire dared not wait any longer, gunning the vehicle back to life.

He sped on, looking around at the remains of his squad, until he realized the gunfire had stopped. The bullet that hit Dog had been the last shot. His dedication to his men, to not wanting to leave anyone behind, had cost Dog his life. As hard a man as he was, Crossfire knew he would feel guilty and be haunted by this decision for the rest of his days. Someone was going to pay for this. Pay dearly.

As he threw the truck into gear, he looked up and saw he was surrounded by close to twenty men aiming machine guns at him. His first instinct was to hit the gas and mow them down regardless of the consequences, but he thought better of it and slowed the truck down. In seconds he had stopped. Quickly, he reached over and removed the dog-tags from each member of Devil Company and stuffed them into his pocket. Despite his current predicament, he knew he would probably live, knew he would escape and find whoever was responsible for the destruction of his platoon and the failure of this mission.

He exited the truck, his hands raised in surrender. As soon as his feet hit the dirt the armed men came on him from every direction. He recognized their uniforms as Iraqi, and now, totally confused, had trouble countenancing the idea of being held by the Iraqi army when he'd been captured trying to escape in a private American company truck. His mind whirled. What had happened? What was a Latham Industries truck doing there? He had to find out. He wouldn't let his men die for nothing.

As he pondered those perplexing questions, something hard crashed into the back of his skull. He fell to the ground and, with darkness looming, heard the Iraqi soldiers discussing his fate.

~ Chapter 2 ~

METRO CITY - PRESENT DAY

The explosion rocked Metro City like an earthquake. Concrete, steel, and glass were pushed into the sky by the fiery hand of the blast. The Wraith stood high atop the Metro City Gallery and watched the fire and smoke billow into the sky. As The Wraith watched over the city, it was quite easy to see and feel the force of the detonation three blocks away.

"Max, do you have a visual on the building that just got hit?" Leena, dressed as The Wraith, said pushing at the transmitter embedded into her cowl.

"Give me a second. I've got it Leena. The explosion came from the Latham Logistics building. From the looks of it, the blast has almost completely obliterated it," Max Horton said over the radio.

"That's not far from my current location. I'm going to get a closer look. Let Paul know that *my* suspect lost me," Leena said, as she broke off into a run and leapt across the roof and onto the adjacent building.

"Be careful. I'll be right behind you on the ground," Max said.

* * * * * *

The Wraith stalked his quarry like a giant nocturnal bird of prey. He knew that Leena, halfway across the city, was following the other suspect. She often dressed as The Wraith, in a costume especially designed by Max to hide her gender, when Paul needed to be in two places at once. As always, she was more than capable of taking care of herself.

The Wraith had received vague information regarding terrorist activity from a small-time jewelry thief he'd captured the previous week. The thief had given up everyone and everything he knew when The Wraith questioned him. Knowing that Robert Latham, the crime lord who presided over everything that was evil in Metro City, had been keeping his criminal activities to an absolute and unusual minimum, so he knew Latham just had to be up to something. He just had to find out, after all this was *his* city to protect.

While the thief had no information on Latham, he had mentioned two men—Eddie Palmer and Joey "Heels" Estalido —who might know something about a possible terrorist plot taking place in Metro City. The Wraith had heard of both men thanks to their previous crimes, but it took a while to track them down, as they had been successfully lying low.

Once they had tracked them down, Leena suggested they each follow one. The Wraith had readily agreed. Both men lived in the same vicinity, so he and Leena could start close together and trail them as the night went on.

When they found them wandering the streets, the men had separated shortly afterwards, just as Leena had predicted, though The Wraith had no idea why they had done so. She was extremely proficient at anticipating criminal behavior, a trait The Wraith had recognized when she began her training with him. However, something about the situation didn't seem right and The Wraith had reservations. He guessed that if something was going on between them, they would not want to be seen together and they would venture to different areas of the city. But it was too late to back out now, and he continued tracking his man. Ultimately, he wondered how this all tied in to Robert Latham. He knew Latham was behind every venomous act in Metro City.

The Wraith stalked Joey Estalido, the more dangerous of the two criminals, from the sky. He circled him from the rooftops above, watching him like a hawk would a mouse. As they made their way across the east end of Metro City the explosion hit. It rocked his very footing and almost sent him crashing to the ground. Looking out across the city, The Wraith saw a fireball shoot straight into the sky. He immediately knew he had tailed the wrong man and that Leena could be in danger. It had definitely been a set-up.

"Leena, Max, are you all right?" Paul said as he pushed the microphone embedded into his cowl.

* * * * * *

Leena sprinted from rooftop to rooftop in the darkness toward the remains of the Latham Logistics building. Having trained to be The Wraith's equal, she was used to the physicality of the job and tonight was no different in that respect. Dressed as The Wraith, Leena leaped with a grace and agility rarely seen in any Olympic sport.

When she first learned that her longtime boyfriend Michael Reeve had taken over the mantle of The Wraith and Paul Sanderson from the original Paul Sanderson, who had been a millionaire recluse, she had no idea how her life would change. Over the last couple of years, her training was put to the test as Metro City was challenged by such dangerous criminals as the Cobra, Natalya Blackova and Magnus Khan. Overcoming those adversaries had taken its toll on them, and the city, and now it looked like more trouble was brewing.

Could this be the terrorist attack Paul was concerned about?

That possibility chilled her to the core.

As she neared the site of the destruction, she could feel the immense heat from the raging inferno, causing her to back away somewhat from the edge of the building she was standing upon. Intense, chunky fumes from the burning wreckage burned her eyes and caused them to slightly water. Narrowing her teary eyes, and standing as close as she could bear without being seen, she strained to see through the heat waves created in the destruction.

"Leena, Max, are you okay?" Paul said over the radio in her ear.

"We're fine, Paul," Leena casually returned as she stared in disbelief at the carnage in front of her.

"I need you to rendezvous with Max and make your way home. That place will be crawling with police and rescue teams soon. There's no use in being seen near there," he said over the radio. "I'll be there shortly."

"Roger that. I'll just take a few pictures while I'm here."

Leena produced an extremely miniature camera from her belt, yet another of Max's innovations. Overlooking the partially destroyed building, she trained the device on the carnage wrought before her and took multiple shots from a variety of angles. From what she remembered of the structure while it was intact, the top five or so stories had taken the most damage in the blast. The building was starting to cave in and she was eerily reminded of 9/11 and the feeling she had when she watched the World Trade Center building collapse on television. Flames belched from the center and an acrid, black smoke began to further fan out into the night air. The building's remaining windows had all been shattered, and the sound of distant sirens now came to her ears.

She wondered how many lives had been lost in this horrendous assault. It was night, so that would have kept the numbers lower than it otherwise might have been had the attack occurred during the day. And the surrounding buildings, including the one she was standing upon, were slightly scorched, but ultimately unscathed. That couldn't have been through sheer luck, Leena thought. Someone skillful was at work here.

And that thought frightened her.

* * * * * *

"I don't believe it! Who would have the audacity to pull something like this?" Robert Latham, the city's biggest industrialist and head of the largest crime cartel on the eastern seaboard, screamed from across his desk. From thirty stories up, Metro City looked tiny from his office window. The city lights shimmered and flickered like Christmas decorations on the tree far below him.

Charlie Grieco, Latham's right-hand man, sat across from him completely speechless. His face was puzzled and only a small whimper of air escaped when he tried to speak to his irate boss.

"That division brought in millions in profits last quarter and was this city's largest supplier of electrical goods," Latham continued. "Trust me, Charlie...someone's head will roll for this!"

Latham's face flushed with anger and he felt the veins throbbing in his forehead. He was beyond mad. He wanted answers. And vengeance. Nobody did this to him and lived to talk about it. In fact, no one had ever done anything to him like this before. Not even Ma Tzi, the Hong Kong drug lord who recently made a failed attempt at taking over Latham's empire in Metro City. He died at Latham's hand in the attempt.

"Sir, we'll find whoever did this," Grieco said as Latham took a deep breath.

"What are you waiting for then? Get out there and bring me the head of..." Latham shouted, but was interrupted by his office door swinging wide open to reveal a large intimidating man aiming a high-powered pistol straight at him.

Grieco spun around in his chair and froze at the sight of the stranger. An instant later, Grieco drew his own pistol from its shoulder harness. Before he could even raise the gun to aim, a single gunshot rang out and the pistol flew from his hand. Grieco appeared unharmed by the stranger's uncannily accurate shot, having hit the pistol and not Grieco's hand.

"That's not a very good idea," the stranger said as he stepped into Latham's office.

Despite the stranger's accuracy, pain was clearly evident on Grieco's face. As his deputy shook his hand and wrist, Latham couldn't help but think that whoever this man was, he was an excellent shot. Latham slowly rose to his feet and leaned forward with his hands on his antique mahogany desk. He smiled at the stranger, though he was seething inside. Feelings of hatred and disdain coursed through him, and although he was smiling, he was as angry as he had ever been in his life.

"Robert Latham, I destroyed your building tonight," the stranger said as he slowly walked across Latham's office.

Latham held his tongue briefly until he could gather his composure. "Just who are you?" he said finally through gritted teeth.

Stepping into the brighter light alongside Grieco, Latham saw exactly how large and menacing the man was. His face was chiseled with scars and it had a blank, emotionless expression of death. For a split second, he thought the man could crush him with his bare hands. He suppressed that notion as quickly as it had come and stared the man down with an intensity he reserved for only the strongest of enemies.

"You can call me...Crossfire," the stranger said as he approached Latham's desk and sat down beside Grieco.

~ Chapter 3 ~

IRAQ - APRIL 8 2003

Crossfire was quickly rolled from his filthy mattress onto the dusty floor. The explosions, fast and repetitious, literally bounced him awake. Startled from the shaking of the whole prison, he stood up and peered out of the small window in his cell. A small brick was missing from the wall, the window in question, and over the years the view it afforded was his only one of the outside world. Even though this view consisted of an adjacent building and a few more in the distance, knowing there still *was* an outside world gave him hope of escaping this hell. Looking out the narrow opening he saw bombs falling from the sky and, upon impact, they threw splashes of fire, dirt, smoke and debris high into the air. He knew this only meant one thing: Iraq was at war.

Crossfire had spent the last twelve years and five months as a prisoner of the Iraqi government. He'd had enough. No matter what it took, he had to somehow make his escape. Having never spoken a word of his mission in Iraq, the military had chosen to keep his capture quiet. He had been abandoned and left to rot. He had spent each day in prison being beaten, interrogated and starved. He never uttered a single word. He wondered daily why he was never executed, and knowing military protocol, he assumed they kept him alive as a possible bargaining or intimidation tool at a later date. Crossfire knew they had made a mistake not executing him and he vowed to show them just how big a mistake.

As the bombing continued, Crossfire looked around his small cell for anything that could be used as a weapon. The only thing there was a worn out and dirty mattress lying directly on the floor with no blanket or pillow and a small wooden bucket, which served as his toilet. When he was given food, which was usually bread and water, it was slid in through a small hatch at the base of the steel door. The cup was usually plastic and he was never given any utensils. They were smart not to give him anything he could possibly use as a weapon. He was not allowed a shirt, only tattered burlap pants, and he went barefoot. The daily beatings to his upper body and face had created scars that appeared like a sort of deranged map of pain.

Knowing he had nothing to work with, he improvised. Thinking quickly, he began to yell incoherently and hold his head as he squatted beside his bathroom bucket. With all of the confusion and destruction in the city around him, he hoped his plan would work, and his screams would be heard above the surrounding carnage.

After a few moments of yelling, a single guard approached his cell with an AK-47 aimed directly at him through the bars in the door. The guard, speaking with a thick Iraqi accent, told him to quiet down immediately. Crossfire continued, ignoring him.

He eyed the guard through his fingers. After a few moments standing at the cell door and screaming for him to be quiet, the guard opened the door. In one quick motion, before the guard could even walk completely into the cell, Crossfire pounced with the bucket and struck the unsuspecting guard across the face with it. The wood splintered everywhere, blinding the guard. Within three seconds of the cell door being unlocked, Crossfire had killed the guard. He grabbed his automatic rifle, large military knife and prison keys, and then took off down the narrow hallway.

There were very few guards evident. Obviously the bombing outside was causing a major diversion. Still, Crossfire ultimately knew he wouldn't get out alive without creating one of his own. The other prisoners would fit perfectly into his plans for escape. He began to cautiously walk down the hall and unlock the other cell doors, nodding approval to the other prisoners. They were now free. In total, he released eight of them, all of them of different races and origins. He had no idea who they were or why they were imprisoned alongside him, but he didn't care. To him, his survival was the only outcome he would accept.

Every time Crossfire had been removed from his cell, he was hooded, bound, and forcefully dragged around, so he had no idea of the layout of the prison. He had a small notion from counting the sound of guard steps and remembering turns he was forced to make, but wasn't entirely sure how big the prison was. One thing he knew for sure was that the building was all on one level, as they never moved him up or down any stairs. He guessed the whole place was either a small detention facility or a death camp. He hoped it wasn't the latter.

After unlocking the other prisoners, they all charged out of the main doors at the end of the hallway without hesitation. Crossfire heard gunfire, and figured it was most likely some guards taking down the fleeing prisoners. Expecting every scenario imaginable in his quick-thinking mind, he darted to the side of the door with the large knife he took at the ready. A guard rushed in, looked around, and before he knew what hit him, Crossfire covered his mouth with one hand and buried the knife deep into his chest with the other. Before the guard hit the ground, Crossfire was half-way to the other end of the prison hall with a second AK-47 slung over the other shoulder.

Just as he had suspected, the rest of the guards immediately rushed in to secure what was left of the prisoners. What they didn't know was that Crossfire was ready for them and opened fire with one of the procured weapons. After the initial burst from his gun all was soon quiet in the hallway with several guards dead on the floor. He inched his way slowly to the door.

Stepping over several dead guards in the doorway, he walked into a larger room with his gun aimed and readied. The room was empty. Looking around, he noticed a familiar small room off to his right. Glancing in, his blood boiled as he recognized this room as the location of his regular beatings. Turning away from the room, he eyed his surroundings closely. There was only one door left with a small window next to it. He could see that it led outside. Freedom was in his grasp and it had never tasted so good.

But Crossfire wasn't prepared to leave just yet. He wanted what they had taken from him when he first arrived. Even though his belongings had been meager, he wanted them back and was determined to find them. Scrambling furiously through small metal cabinets and lockers, he came up empty handed. Moving to a series of battered, wooden desks, his search ended quickly. In the first desk he came to he found his dog-tags and those that belonged to his fallen Devil Company squad members in the top drawer. He put them all around his neck and started to leave.

Passing an open locker, he caught sight of himself in a small mirror for the first time in years. He looked appalling and realized he couldn't leave looking like he did. The bags under his eyes bespoke of regular sleep deprivation and his face was swollen. He had not shaved in over twelve years, so his beard was long and scraggly. His hair was long, matted and unkempt. He ruefully glared at the dead guards in the doorway and then an idea hit him.

Crossfire eased the door open to the prison, his AK-47 ready at hand. Dressed in an Iraqi soldier's uniform, he was ready to put his plan into action. He just had to make sure not to be noticed.

Stepping out into the daylight, his eyes momentarily stung. He was taken back at the realization as to where he was and what had happened. He instantly recognized his surroundings. He was in Baghdad and Iraq was at war, most likely with the United States, he guessed, but he couldn't be sure. He wondered how and why briefly before snapping back to his mission at hand. Escape. He saw U.S. Air Force jets, confirming his surmise, soaring above the city and dropping pinpoint bomb strikes. They were relentless in their attack. In the distance, he saw U.S. Abrams tanks slowly crawling through the streets with soldiers in tow. Whatever Iraq had done or been involved in, he knew it was time to get out as quickly as he could. His own countrymen were as unwelcome to him now as the enemy.

Thinking quickly, he dashed toward a nearby abandoned marketplace, no doubt so because of the attack on the city. Crossfire quickly eyed the numerous merchant stalls for anything useful. Scanning here and there, he finally found a pair of what appeared to be American style blue jeans and a solid black t-shirt. Knowing it would have to do, he quickly changed behind a stall and darted into a nearby alley. He needed time to think, to formulate a new plan to escape from the war being waged around him.

~ Chapter 4 ~

METRO CITY - PRESENT DAY

"**W**ho was behind the attack?" The Wraith growled.

Joey "Heels" Estalido sat at the end of an alley with his back against the grimy brick wall staring at the two glowing yellow Eyes on The Wraith's chest. He was terrified beyond belief, but knew no matter what he said the masked vigilante wouldn't believe a word. He shook with fear as The Wraith edged closer.

At that instant, Joey knew he would rather go to prison for years than deal with the Dread Avenger any longer. He'd heard stories on the street of what he was capable of doing to criminals and Joey had always hoped he never would cross paths with him. Unfortunately, he had done just that. While he assumed, or rather hoped, most of what he had heard to be rumor, and seeing that The Wraith had only cornered him and nothing more, he still didn't want to push his luck. He tensed and tried to look away but the glowing Eyes drew him in.

"This is your last chance, Estalido. Tell me who was behind the attack and why you and Eddie Palmer were acting as diversions," The Wraith said as he lunged forward and grabbed Joey by the sides of his head.

"I...I don't know who was behind any attack. I swear it! Eddie and I were paid to split up into two different directions and act as diversions in case the police followed us. We honestly didn't even know there was going to be an attack," Joey screamed.

"I don't believe you," The Wraith moaned through clenched teeth as the yellow Eyes on his chest grew brighter.

"I swear it! You gotta believe me, man! This guy gave us a lot of money, told us to just walk across town and nothing would happen to us. He even mapped out where we were to go."

The squeezing of Joey's head, as if he was being gripped in a vice, was momentarily relieved as The Wraith slightly released his grip.

"Who paid you?" The Wraith asked as he again tightened his grip.

"Some guy we both never saw before! He was all scarred up and had a weird tattoo on his neck that looked like crosshairs on a gun's scope. That's all I know," Joey squealed.

The grip on his head tightened and he felt excruciating pressure in his temples. His eyes were forced open and began to bulge out. Joey felt as if his head was literally being crushed like a melon. Then he heard the voice. The most horrifyingly deep and gravelly voice he could ever remember hearing and it seemed as if it came from inside his own head.

"Feel all of the pain and torment you have inflicted on others. Feel all of the suffering you have caused. Your crimes, your sins, and the harm you have caused with every evil choice you've made... Feel it all... Feel your evil returned..."

In an instant Joey understood the voice. He felt the torment he had caused each of his victims both directly and indirectly. The suffering he placed on families stricken by his murderous ways, the pain he had caused from cheating people out of their money and stealing their property, and the evil sickness he'd spread across Metro City wherever he went. He felt it all at once. It was so overwhelming and intense that Joey thought he had died and been condemned to hell where suffering and punishment were regularly given. After what felt like an eternity, but in reality was only seconds, The Wraith dropped him like a sack of potatoes. He breathed heavily, in abject pain, with darkness beckoning.

* * * * * *

When Joey woke up, he found himself handcuffed and sitting in police custody. He had been left on the steps of the Metro City Police Department with a note pinned to his jacket stating he had information relating to the recent terrorist attack.

As he was questioned, Joey told Detective Bob Sloan everything he knew...even about The Wraith. He babbled and moaned about every crime he had ever committed and been involved with. As such, he was held on pending charges and a full investigation. Sloan immediately issued an all-points-bulletin to all patrols for the capture of Eddie Palmer.

Placing him in a quiet cell, Detective Sloan was sure he would need to question him again. Especially about The Wraith.

* * * * * *

Robert Latham sat down and smiled. He looked Crossfire up and down carefully. Shooting Charlie Grieco a quick glance, he saw his deputy still rubbing his hand as he glared his assailant down. Folding his fingers together, he leaned back in his chair and nodded to his newest adversary.

"Well...I'm listening," Latham said as he grinned sardonically.

Crossfire, eyeing Latham intently, drew a pistol from his hip and shoved it directly into Grieco's temple. Latham didn't flinch or appear worried at Crossfire's brazen lack of respect.

"December twenty-second, nineteen ninety," Crossfire said slowly.

"Yeah, okay. What about it?" Latham asked, growing impatient.

"My men and I were hired and dispatched to a small Iraqi town to recover an artifact for the government. Upon arrival, my entire squad was killed and I was imprisoned for over twelve years. We were completely set up. I understand that being in Karbah was risky at that time for anyone. What I don't understand is why your company was there."

Latham studied Crossfire closely. He watched how he spoke, how he moved, how he carried himself. None of that bothered him as much as the fact that the entire time, Crossfire never took his eyes off of him. He hated to admit it made him slightly nervous. He had no idea who Crossfire was and yet this man had some sort of vendetta against him. Deciding not to play into his intimidation game, Latham chose to play the diplomat instead and disavow any knowledge of his company's overseas dealings.

"Look, Latham Industries has contracts all over the world. I'm not sure what you saw, or what you thought you saw, but I can assure you of one thing; neither I, nor my company, had anything to do with your squad's deaths or your imprisonment," Latham calmly stated.

"I have spent the last eight years studying you. I know everything you do and everything your company does. I have watched you and everyone important to you and your company. You are lying to me. I know why you were in Iraq and what you were looking for, but I want to know why my team was set up," Crossfire grunted with building menace.

"I don't know what you're talking about. We've never even met before today. I don't know you or anything about you," Latham bit back.

"Oh, we've met before. You probably just don't remember seeing my face as I crashed your charity benefit a few years back," Crossfire said smiling widely.

"You..." Latham gasped as he remembered that disastrous night.

"Yes. Now, you owe me an explanation for why my team is dead and why we were set up. I gave you something, an explanation as to who was responsible for the attack on your party, so now give me something in return."

Latham, always one step ahead, pressed a security button located under his desk with his foot. Within thirty seconds, his personal bodyguards would appear and Crossfire would be detained, escorted out, and taken care of with extreme prejudice.

"I owe you nothing," he said with menace of his own. "In fact, I respect that you had the intestinal fortitude to obliterate one of my buildings and brazenly burst in here to confront me, but there is something you don't understand," Latham grinned at Crossfire and narrowed his eyes with boastful pride. "I am Robert Latham and you have no idea what I'm capable of or who you're dealing with!"

Crossfire, without warning, lowered his pistol and fired into Grieco's left leg. The gunshot rang out and echoed around the enclosed walls of the office. The sound was deafening but Latham didn't move. He stared Crossfire down with a boiling hatred and knew that any second this man was as good as dead.

* * * * * *

The sound of the gunshot had caused him to flinch but that was nothing compared to the intense, burning sensation and excruciating pain just above his knee. His ears rang from the ballistic explosion and his head pounded in time with each heartbeat.

Screaming out in agony, Grieco slumped from his comfortable plush office chair and, holding his leg, began to writhe in pain on the floor. Just before he hit the ground he caught a glimpse of his boss and could have sworn that Robert Latham was smiling devilishly.

With darkness looming amidst the pain, he swore both men would pay for this terrible and unprovoked assault upon him.

* * * * * *

As Grieco spilled from his chair, Crossfire shifted his eyes back to his new nemesis. Things hadn't gone exactly according to his plan, but his message to Latham was loud and clear, and that's all that mattered. He was going to make him suffer in more ways than he thought imaginable.

Knowing that Latham had a state of the art security system in place, he figured he had mere seconds before a small army of guards came in and opened fire on him. He was right. Hearing the sounds of footsteps behind him about to enter the office, Crossfire resorted to his backup plan.

Turning the pistol on Latham, Crossfire briefly thought about pulling the trigger and ending his vendetta, but wanted him to suffer more. This wasn't the time for revenge. He was going to show Latham he was here to stay and he was going to be a thorn in his side.

"Do it! Do it, coward!" Latham gnashed through closed teeth. His vicious and evil face shone through the shadows and gave Crossfire a glimpse of Latham's true persona.

Crossfire moved the pistol slightly to his right and fired three times. Latham never moved and continued to glare at him. The window behind Latham fragmented into shards as the bullets tore through its double-paned thickness.

In the blink of an eye, Crossfire hopped across Latham's desk and dove out of the window behind him. He fell into the darkness and disappeared into the night.

* * * * * *

Latham rushed to the window. There was no sign of Crossfire. Turning back around and glancing down at Grieco, Latham's guards entered the office with their weapons at the ready. As usual, they were too late.

"Mr. Grieco has been unfortunately injured. Call an ambulance for him please," Latham casually instructed the guards.

For an instant Latham thought that he had underestimated this new menace. He hadn't. Something about Crossfire commanded his respect. If he could somehow pit Crossfire against his other great enemy, The Wraith, that could potentially solve both his problems. But how? That became the question that burned in his mind. How? He had to think, to formulate some sort of plan. It was just one more step in his plan for total control of Metro City and he knew no one would be able to stop him then.

Not even...

The Wraith.

~ Chapter 5 ~

When Detective Bob Sloan finally reached his desk after an extremely long night, he was relieved to be able to sit down and collect his thoughts. It had been a rough night of explosions, questioning people, and confronting yet more rumors of The Wraith spreading his form of vigilante justice across the city. He was exhausted and the dark circles under his eyes that morning suggested he was ready for a vacation, but vacationing while his city was systematically being flushed down the drain was *not* an option. His work was also piling up all around him and he felt Metro City, despite all of his hard work, was falling further into chaos.

Looking at the clock, he realized it was almost time for his shift to start, although he hadn't actually stopped working since the day before. Double overtime. Extremely irritable, he fidgeted about as he welcomed the sight of his partner,

Detective Rosa Perez, with a broad and warm smile as she sat down across from him.

"Let me guess...been here all night?" she asked as she slid him a piping hot cup of coffee.

Sloan nodded and smiled as he sipped the coffee.

"You have to sleep sometime. Even the criminals sleep," she chided him.

"Yeah, but this city doesn't," he bit back as he scalded his tongue on the hot beverage.

Sloan looked up and saw Perez staring at him with a mixture of respect and annoyance. She was the only one on the whole force that he felt understood him. She knew his workaholic ways and still admired him for it. Sloan smiled weakly back at her and sipped gently at his coffee.

"Sorry. I'm just tired. This is perfect. Thanks."

Sloan admired Perez as much as she did him. She was attractive, in an average sort of way, and he found her Latin heritage an extra incentive to her overall charm. There was an unspoken honor between them and, apart from his wife; she was the only woman he truly trusted.

"Well, let's get on with it then," Sloan said. "We've got a lot to go over. From the terrorist attack to The Wraith, we have a lot of work piling up."

"The Wraith?" Perez asked almost spitting her coffee out.

Sloan just looked at her solemnly and nodded. Grabbing a large stack of files, he handed them to her and smiled.

"Where would you like to start?" he said pointedly.

* * * * * *

In the Lair, located within the center of Sanderson House, the inner city mansion home of Paul Sanderson, Paul sat at his computer staring at the screen and shaking his head in disbelief. Studying a detailed three-dimensional readout of Metro City that he could move and manipulate with a gentle finger movement, he tapped the screen and then moved his thumb and index fingers apart. The Latham Logistics building and surrounding area magnified on the screen.

"I just don't get it. Why was that building hit?" Paul asked as he spun his chair around to face Leena.

Leena sat just behind Paul at another computer console deep in thought. He recognized the mug shots displayed on her monitor, after all he was responsible for most of their arrests or captures.

"I'm thinking it was a message," Leena said finally, spinning around in her chair to face Paul. "A vendetta against Robert Latham."

"I thought that too, but why was that specific building targeted? I'm sure it holds some sort of significance," Paul said as he slumped in his chair and scratched his head.

He was rarely stumped like this but the previous day's events made absolutely no sense to him. None of his snitches or operatives knew anything of value and the problem was gnawing at him. Nobody decimated an entire building, taking countless lives, in his city and got away with it.

"Leena, can you run a financial report on Latham Logistics?" he said finally, acting on a hunch.

Leena nodded and spun back around to her computer. Paul heard tapping from her keyboard as he turned back to look at the map. Robert Latham owned buildings all over Metro City, but Paul couldn't fathom why that particular building had been destroyed. There were several buildings that could have been taken out, and if the vendetta angle was true, surely his personal office tower would have been the better option.

"Latham Logistics turned the highest profit of all Latham Industries divisions in the last year. It was the only section of his business that more than tripled its assets for the entire fiscal year. It generated over two billion dollars in profit alone," Leena read from her monitor.

Paul stood and walked over to get a closer look at her screen. As he stood and read over the numbers, he couldn't help but wonder how all of this stacked up and how Latham played into it. Something struck Paul as he read and he immediately focused solely on the screen.

"There! That could be something," he said pointing to the screen.

"Iraq?" Leena asked curiously. "I don't understand."

"It's a good possibility that someone overseas has it in for Latham and decided to strike him at the heart of his most profitable division."

It wasn't much, but it was all they had and it was a place to pinpoint further investigation. He walked back to his computer and sat down. Instantly he began manipulating his screen to show him more detailed information on Latham Industries.

"See if you can continue to find a connection between those two criminals we tailed and Robert Latham. I have an idea," he said.

"Already on it," Leena said giving him the thumbs up.

* * * * * *

Robert Latham stood in front of what used to be the Latham Logistics building. Its smoldering wreckage was the only evidence of a once profitable business division. As he stood there steaming inside, he couldn't help but feel some small measure of respect for Crossfire. He recognized that only the most powerful of adversaries could achieve what he had, and that had to be respected, if not admired.

The myriad press members clambered behind him trying to get any information from him that they could, but Latham chose to ignore them. To him the press was merely a pawn for him to use as he saw fit. Ultimately, he controlled what they released about him or his organization, and right now, silence served him best. He needed time to think, to ascertain Crossfire's next move and determine a way to turn it to his advantage. Gaining this advantage would allow him to expand his cartel further and rightfully deal with anyone who stood in his way.

Backing away from his destroyed building, Latham put on his best face for the photographers. It was easy for him to put on a display of remorse and despair and he knew everyone would fall for it. To him people were mindless sheep and they needed him to herd them into his new era of control and absolute power.

As he walked slowly to his limousine, the myriad photographers and cameramen snapped their photos and took their video footage for their news stories. Inside, he knew he had everyone right where he wanted them. He was in control and loved every second of it. Not everyone was in his grasp, though. He still had Crossfire and The Wraith to figure into his plan. No matter who was defeated between them, he would be less one enemy and that made him smile. To the public, his smile was one of sadness and perhaps a little hope, but inside the smile was venomous and contemptuous.

His hatred for Crossfire and The Wraith was unparalleled. His ultimate goal now was to destroy them both, but he figured they would cross paths soon enough. He then could stand back hoping each would kill the other in the struggle and he would emerge the victor. When all was said and done, Latham would be the city's savior.

They would see the mess they were left in the destructive wake of the fight between the Crossfire and The Wraith, he thought, and they would need him. They would beg him to take the reins and lead them out of the darkness.

They just didn't know it yet.

* * * * * *

Slowly coming to and rubbing the sleep from his eyes, Charlie Grieco remembered very little. Looking around, he realized he was in a hospital bed and had various tubes and sensors hooked up to his arms and chest. Moving slightly, he tugged at the oxygen tubing running into his nostrils. The room was dark except for the slight slivers of light creeping through the closed blinds on the window. All save the heart monitor, and other equipment, the world around him was silent.

The last thing he remembered was severe pain in his leg and the sounds of gunfire and glass shattering. Quickly, it all came back to him. Anger surged through him as he remembered Crossfire holding a gun to his temple and then shooting him in the leg. He glanced down and saw his wound heavily bandaged.

He struggled to get up on his elbow so he could sit up. His leg felt numb and slightly sore. He was very uncomfortable in his present position. As he looked around the room, he heard a slight rustle in the darkest corner. Grieco strained his eyes in that direction but saw nothing. He listened hard but only the faint sounds of his morphine drip, oxygen supplier, and various monitors could be heard. Thinking he must have imagined it, he settled back down.

Feeling drowsy, he suddenly caught sight of something. Out of the darkness came a large figure toward him.

"Hello, Mr. Grieco," the figure said.

Bolting upright in his bed, Grieco saw Crossfire step out of the darkness and approach him. A wave of fear and anger coursed through his veins as he stared at him in disbelief.

"We have a few things to discuss about your boss," Crossfire said casually.

Grieco reached for the call button on the monitor, but heard a loud metallic click before he could press it. A large handgun was aimed directly at him. Thinking better of it, he slumped back down in the bed and glared at Crossfire with contempt.

"That's better. Now, how about you tell me about this coin and why Robert Latham wants it so badly."

Grieco looked on as Crossfire produced a large, golden coin in his other hand. It was ornately decorated and appeared very old. It was absolutely beautiful, shining hypnotically in the low light. Oddly enough, he wanted to hold it, caress it. For a brief moment, it was all he could think about.

"I've never seen that before in my life," Grieco told him blankly but truthfully.

"I figured you'd say that," Crossfire said as he pocketed the coin and approached his bed.

~ Chapter 6 ~

METRO CITY – AUGUST 10 2006

The traffic was horrific. An accident involving a large passenger bus and a small sedan had the interstate running along Metro City at a stand-still. People stood around everywhere watching as emergency response crews and police tried to untangle the wreckage. With the exit ramp in sight in the distance, and the damage from the accident extensive, Crossfire knew it would be a very long time before police could clear the route.

Crossfire had rented a small cargo van in Miami and driven it virtually across the country to pick up various supplies before returning to the east coast to Metro City. The inside of the van had been filled with wooden cargo crates and small metal lock boxes.

As he waited in the traffic jam, Crossfire began to mull over his options. Swiping a small laptop from the passenger seat, he wanted to search the local classifieds for what might serve as his base of operations. With a satellite card inserted, he began browsing the Internet for listings.

Surprisingly, he was able to quickly find what he was looking for. Sliding his finger around the small touchpad, he saw pictures of his new residence spin on the screen in front of him. It was perfect and would be right under the nose of his enemy.

The traffic finally started to move after another hour or so. With the laptop open in the seat beside him, he grabbed a disposable mobile phone he had purchased at a gas station and dialed the number from the listing. Waiting for an answer, Crossfire navigated the traffic and took the off-ramp exit into the city.

"Hello, Latham Industries, realty division, how may I direct your call?" the pleasant female voice over the phone answered.

"I'm interested in the harbor warehouse lease," Crossfire said smiling.

* * * * * *

The building was very spacious and ideal for his needs. Looking around it, Crossfire decided that this warehouse would be perfect for him, and the irony of renting it from a Latham Industries subsidiary only made it more so. Robert Latham would soon pay, and his desired outcome was slowly coming to fruition.

Pulling a rolled stack of cash from his jacket, he smiled as he thumbed through it, distracting the real estate agent with it.

"When can I move in?" he asked.

Enticed by the large roll of money, the agent grinned widely at him. "Well, there are lease fees, deposits, and insurance premiums that must be paid up front on top of the yearly lease rate. I'm sure I can expedite this for you if you're ready this week."

"How much will it cost to get me in today?" he asked as he thumbed the money, causing a ruffling paper sound.

*   *   *   *   *   *

Crossfire was right to believe that money talked, particularly in Latham's world. He immediately pulled out his savings from an old safety deposit box to get started. Almost immediately, he realized his plan was going to cost more than originally planned, as the economy had changed dramatically during his imprisonment. With a money truck waylaid here and a bank robbed there, he soon saw his funds increase in no time at all. If money were his sole objective, he could be a millionaire many times over but money was merely the means to an end for him. The life he once wanted and set out to achieve was gone. All of his hopes for Devil Company, his retirement, and the quiet last few years he wanted for his life had been stripped away. Now he existed only for revenge. Nothing else mattered.

Registering under the name Randy Ennis, he was able to convince the real estate agent that it was imperative that he move in immediately to set up his business. Negotiating the paperwork was easy; he slipped her a hundred dollar bill each time she questioned him about something. His story was he wanted to move in immediately because he was an Internet dealer on a famous auction website and needed a place to store and ship his wares. Within twenty minutes the paperwork was signed and he was the new occupant of an old waterfront Latham-owned warehouse. The location was perfect as the harbor provided a potential escape route should things go amiss. Every contingency had to be meticulously planned for—his mission was too important.

After the agent had left him at his new property, Crossfire began unpacking his van. The first thing he did was to install his personalized state of the art security system. He needed to get as close to Robert Latham as possible, but as he set up the security system he reasoned his current task would probably be the more difficult of the two.

* * * * * *

Walking into Latham's office, Charlie Grieco couldn't help but feel apprehensive. He hated giving bad news to his boss. It wasn't uncommon for Latham to take out his frustration on his employees and he knew this could be one of those times if it went badly. He hated his boss for a number of reasons, but this side of Latham most of all.

Gently wrapping on the door frame with his knuckles, Grieco waited for Latham to acknowledge him before entering. He hated the fact that he was merely a lackey and a pawn to be used as Latham saw fit. He may be Latham's right-hand man, but one wouldn't know it from the treatment he often endured. Grieco saw Latham as a self-centered egomaniac and he silently vowed to take him out when the timing was perfect. Until then, he would be the yes-man Latham needed and use his position to get close enough to drive the proverbial knife deep into his boss's back.

Looking up from his phone call, Latham beckoned Grieco in with a casual wave. Bracing himself, Grieco kept his emotions in check, eased into the large office and took a seat.

"...and thanks again for the information," Latham said, beaming, as he hung up the phone and looked up at Grieco.

"We have a situation," Grieco said softly, wondering when his boss' anger would start to boil over.

"Do tell, Charlie," Latham said, stony faced, as he leaned back in his leather chair.

"There is a Detective Sloan downstairs. He says he's here investigating some report that you may have ties to an Afghan smuggling ring," Grieco said, again softly.

"Well, that kind of assumption is never good, Charlie. Go ahead and send him up," Latham said casually as he spun his chair to face the giant window behind him.

Knowing he had been dismissed, Grieco stood up and begrudgingly walked out of the office. To Latham, loyalty could be bought and sold at a whim. That was evident based on the frequent times he had failed to trust Grieco with information. As he walked out of the office, Grieco reminded himself to keep his cool and wait patiently. He knew that Latham would ultimately be his own undoing, so waiting for the right time to strike was a concept he had made peace with long ago.

Waiting was something he was exceptionally good at.

* * * * * *

Crossfire had spent most of the afternoon and evening installing his security system. When it was finished he began laying out his equipment and weapons. Checking everything over, he felt like he was preparing for war and he certainly had enough weapons and ammunition to supply a small army. There were machine guns, handguns, assault rifles, grenades and rocket launchers; Crossfire was about to declare war on Robert Latham. Grabbing his favorite weapon, a fully customized Smith & Wesson 4506-1 .45 ACP with a laser sight, he cocked it and sat it down next to its identical mate. He checked his inventory again and made notes in regards to the supplies he had and those he still needed.

He glanced over at a newspaper he had picked up on his way into Metro City. The front-page headline piqued his curiosity:

MASKED VIGILANTE TERRORIZES METRO CITY

He browsed through the article about a mysterious crime-fighter known only to Metro City's underworld as The Wraith. He chuckled at the absurdity of it and figured someone had been watching too much television.

Dismissing the article as a joke, he began to flip through the paper looking for any further information on Latham. He didn't have to look far as the second page he turned to was a full page spread titled:

ROBERT LATHAM TO RECEIVE HUMANITY AWARD AT BENEFIT

His mind swirled with ideas as he read on. The benefit dinner would be held at the Metro City Hospice Center and was by invitation only. Noting the date, he saw he had one day to prepare.

Crossfire smiled devilishly as he realized just how impeccable the timing of his arrival in Metro City had been. Closing the paper, he looked again at the front page. A pitiful police sketch of The Wraith was the centerpiece of the speculative article. Crossfire's smile widened even more.

This is going to be so easy, he thought. *Almost too easy.*

~ Chapter 7 ~

METRO CITY – PRESENT DAY

Paul Sanderson looked up from his morning paper to see Leena slide into the sizeable breakfast nook across from him. Smiling gently at her, he couldn't help but realize how beautiful she looked in the morning sun as it crept through the windows.

As they sat exchanging loving glances, their butler Jonathan Simpson gracefully placed a breakfast tray between them. Coffee, fruit juice, milk, fresh fruit, and lightly toasted bread covered the ornate, silver tray. Nodding their approval, they continued to stare at one another as Simpson excused himself and went about his daily duties.

"I think I've finally made the connection between Latham and Iraq," Paul said as he grabbed an apple and sat back comfortably. "During the first Gulf War, he contracted a division of Latham Industries out to the U.S. government to help stockpile supplies in various regions. According to reports, it was mainly food and medicine to assist the military as they were stationed and deployed."

"Okay, but I'm sure someone wouldn't target him for just giving government aid," Leena said.

"Right. So, after some further digging, I found out that the U.S. ended his contract abruptly after he reported several of his trucks missing. They were recovered by U.S. troops months later in a small border village called Karbah. According to the report, Latham had dealings with the locals there, but their nature could never be determined or proven. The strange thing about it all is that Latham Industries report leaving Karbah six months after the military contract ended."

"So, you think Latham had something going on there he didn't want the government to know about and used the supplies and aid as cover to legally enter that area?" Leena asked as she leaned forward and intently awaited Paul's response.

"I do. I don't know what he was doing there, but I know he wouldn't be there, especially in the middle of a war, unless he could profit by it."

As they sat silently and mulled over the situation, Leena suddenly looked around curiously.

"Paul...where's Max?"

* * * * * *

As Max came to, he eyed his darkened surroundings as best he could. Feeling a stretched, burning sensation in his arms and wrists, Max looked up to see he was tied and bound to a large iron hook embedded in the ceiling above him. His toes barely touched the ground and he felt as if his shoulders were about to pull free from their sockets. He noticed his shirt had been removed and he had a rope around his ankles binding them together.

Remembering nothing of what had happened, and not knowing where he was, he looked around to gain any bearings he could. He couldn't see much in the near-darkness that surrounded him, but at the opposite end of the spacious room he saw a very large man sitting at a workbench beneath a small light that had been suspended from the ceiling. The light flickered eerily, casting ominous shadows on the bulk of the man. He had his back to Max and appeared to be working on something on the bench.

"Hey!" Max yelled at him.

The man stood slowly and turned to face him, but the only light in the room was behind him and Max suddenly feared what this shadowy man would do to him. As he walked closer, Max's eyes adjusted and he got a better look. He tried to take in as much detail about the man as possible. He was above average in height but extremely muscular. His entire face was scarred and it looked as if it had seen a lot of punishment. His salt and pepper colored hair was shoulder length and was pulled back into a slick pony tail that danced gently across his neck and shoulders as he walked.

He approached silently and this concerned Max even more. Stepping close enough to look him in the eyes, Max noticed a faded tattoo on his neck. It looked like crosshairs, but he wasn't totally sure in the low light. Regardless, the man and his presence made Max feel unsettled.

Without a word uttered, the man delivered a devastating right hook to Max's jaw. It sent a shockwave of pain through his entire body and caused his senses to go haywire. His vision blurred and he felt himself about to pass out, but he hung on. A coppery taste built up in his mouth and he knew that this brute had busted his mouth open. Taking a moment to draw the blood around his tongue, Max spat it out into his kidnapper's face.

"Whatta ye want with me?" Max asked, his voice filled with rage.

The man said nothing and smiled as he wiped the blood from his cheek. His retaliation was so fast, Max didn't see the next hit coming. A left hook smashed the other side of his face and the intense pain returned. He couldn't remember ever being hit so hard in his life. His head felt too heavy for his neck and he felt his chin bounce slightly off of his chest. Opening his eyes was too much for him and he began to drift into unconsciousness.

As the darkness enveloped Max, his last thought was that this sadistic man enjoyed inflicting pain.

* * * * * *

Walking toward his workbench, Crossfire wiped the rest of the blood from his face with a dirty towel. Sitting down, he resumed equipping an unusually large scope on an automatic rifle. Moments later a loud squelch and then static emitted from a small, high-tech communicator sitting directly beside him.

"Max, come in. Are you there? Repeat...Max, come in. Are you there?" a deep and gravelly voice said over the transmitter.

Crossfire stared at the communicator before turning to look at Max, who hung unconscious behind him. Turning back to the small device, Crossfire snatched it up and clicked the button on the side.

"Max is...indisposed at the moment."

The speaker squawked again and the same voice spoke.

"Who is this and what have you done with Max?"

"I'm the man who leveled Latham Logistics yesterday. I've come to this city to destroy Robert Latham, and I've only begun to make him suffer. Your friend is safe... for now. You have my word that he will return to you safely as long as you —"

"You will let him go now!" the voice growled, cutting Crossfire abruptly off.

"I'm sorry, Wraith, but he's my insurance policy. It has to be this way so you'll stay out of my way," he said.

There was a long pause as Crossfire stared at the communicator intently. He wanted a response and he seemed to beg the little transmitter for a reply. He knew that The Wraith would try to stop him and wouldn't let him take Latham down *his* way. From what he had read in the papers he knew the vigilante was honorable and wouldn't agree with his methods, but it had to be *his* way if Latham was to pay. After what seemed like an eternity, the voice responded.

"I'll find you. I'll find out who you are and take you down. This is *my* city and you can't hide for long," The Wraith said harshly.

"Are you challenging me, Wraith?" Crossfire shot back.

"It's a promise!"

The communicator went dead and it took a moment for Crossfire to realize The Wraith had had the last word. This wasn't over between them, but he knew he had other business to attend to first. He really didn't care for The Wraith or his mission to cleanse the city of its crime. All that mattered to him was revenge.

However, by kidnapping The Wraith's aide, he realized he may have started a war he hadn't planned. He just wanted The Wraith to stay out of the way so his plans against

Latham could come to full fruition. Max was merely a pawn to ensure The Wraith listened and obeyed. Thinking over the conversation, he wondered if he'd made an enemy he didn't want or need, but it had to be so. If The Wraith tried to stop him, he knew what he had to do.

As he stared at the communicator deep in thought, Crossfire heard Max stir behind him. Crossfire knew The Wraith and his team were very resourceful. He couldn't have Max trying to escape or signal anyone. Nothing must stop him from wreaking vengeance upon Latham. *Nothing.*

"He'll come for you..." Max coughed out as blood dribbled from his mouth and onto his chest.

Walking toward Max, Crossfire shook his head and smiled.

"You better hope and pray he doesn't."

~ Chapter 8 ~

METRO CITY - AUGUST 11 2006

Bob Sloan groaned to himself as he looked around the room of politicians, businessmen, and wealthy industrialists. The charity benefit was to honor Robert Latham for his generous contributions to various aid organizations. All of the secretive winks and nods disgusted him. He couldn't help but feel as if this was just a big exercise in stroking the egos of the wealthy. From the corner of his eye he saw his boss, Commissioner George Harrison, walking toward him.

Sloan always regarded Harrison as a great man of integrity. With most of the police force corrupt, in the pocket of Latham or others, he felt that Harrison always did the best he could to maintain a sense of balance within Metro City. Knowing he had to be there as a representative council member, Sloan wondered if this event made Harrison's stomach turn as much as his own.

"Bob," Harrison greeted. I didn't know you were on the guest list," he said pointedly.

"I'm not. I'm here on business, sir."

Harrison put his arm around Sloan and leaned in close. "Bob, listen to me. We both know why you're here, but keep your distance from Latham. The man is dangerous and if he feels you're trying to muscle him or spy on him...well, let's just say I need you alive."

Sloan thought briefly. He smiled and nodded in agreement. He would never question his boss, nor would he attempt to publicly make him look bad or risk an investigation. He extended his hand for Harrison to shake.

"I understand, sir. How about I take a seat and just watch the reception?"

Harrison took Sloan's hand and smiled. Sloan always thought his boss had a warm and comforting smile, and no matter what the situation was, he felt as if the man was always genuine.

"Good idea. Keep well back but with your eyes open."

With that, Harrison turned into the crowd and began politely shaking hands and casually speaking to random people as he headed toward his seat. Sloan felt awkward in such a crowd, especially in his cheap, rented tux. He turned to look for a seat near the back of the auditorium. Making waves was something he did from time to time, but he realized tonight was not the night for such shenanigans.

Looking around, he saw notable and prominent figures from the highest echelons of society. Robert Latham sat poised in the center of a long table near the front with the likes of the mayor, industrialist and business tycoon Edward Truman and, surprisingly enough, millionaire playboy Paul

Sanderson. The table was an eclectic mix of money and power and Sloan couldn't help but briefly feel insignificant amongst the elite of the city. He chided himself for such feelings, momentary as they were. He was as good, if not better, than anyone in this room and he knew it.

Sloan spotted an empty seat at a table amongst several elderly women who were no doubt filthy rich. He nodded to them and slipped casually into the chair. They halted their heated conversation about who was the most charitable among them, watched Sloan slide into his chair with contempt and then resumed their argument.

Feeling that strange sensation as if someone was staring at him, Sloan glanced around the vast ballroom. He spied Robert Latham eyeing him intently from the front of the room. Noticing Sloan had caught his eye, Latham delivered a wide grin followed by a slow wink. Forcing himself not to glare back, Sloan slowly looked away.

He was out of place and extremely uncomfortable in such an environment, and he wondered if it had been a smart idea to attend in the first place. Now he had an overwhelming urge to leave. He was used to daily dealings with low-life murderers, pimps, thieves and drug-dealers on the streets; he realized now he was still among the same type of people except they were wearing tuxes and gowns. Excusing himself from the table, he smiled at the elderly ladies. Walking across the room, he decided to head out to the veranda for some fresh air.

* * * * * *

The hallways were largely clear in the Metro City Hospice Center save for a few people here and there searching for an exit or restroom. As Crossfire navigated the halls toward the

ballroom, he knew this was going to be a night Robert
Latham would never forget.

* * * * * *

Robert Latham accepted his charity award for hospitality
and smiled for the many photographers. Waving to the
crowd, he proudly held up his award and smiled broadly. The
camera flashes were momentarily blinding. He motioned
with his hand for silence, cleared his throat and began to
speak.

"First off, I'd like to thank Metro City. You are the
greatest city in the world and it's my daily goal to give back
to the city that has allowed Latham Industries to grow and
succeed."

The cameras flashed intensely as he was interrupted by a
roar of applause and cheers.

"Every dime we make is due to the great people of this
city, so giving back is something I don't even have to think
about doing. I simply do it. It gives me such pleasure to look
out and see Latham Industries helping so many people and
changing so many lives."

The applause was deafening. Latham, smiling widely and
eating up the attention, motioned for the crowd to allow him
to continue.

"Secondly, I'd like to thank all of the committees and
councils represented here tonight. As my peers, your support
and recognition means so much to me...and your friendship
means even more. So, I humbly accept this award on behalf
of Latham Industries and promise that we will continue to
give back each and every day. Thank you."

Latham posed for the cameras and nodded to random
people spread across the room. As he stood in the limelight

holding his award, he noticed Bob Sloan standing by the veranda door at the back of the ballroom. Sloan was glaring at him with disdain. Graciously accepting the praise from everyone in the room, Latham gave a slight nod and smile to Sloan as if to say he was untouchable and ruled this city with an iron fist. Seeing that he got the message, Latham eyed Sloan as the police detective turned his back and walked outside onto the veranda.

Giving a final wave, Latham stood there a little longer just to savor the praise. When he finally sat down, he felt as if he had everyone right where he wanted them. Sure, there were a few police officers on the force, like Bob Sloan, that couldn't be bought, but they were the minority and therefore beyond thinking about. The Wraith, however, was another matter entirely. To be rid of him, he thought, he would do almost anything.

* * * * * *

Unconscious kitchen staff littered the floor around Crossfire's feet. He grabbed a ski-mask from his small bag, pulled it over his head and adjusted it so he could see. Then he wrapped a long black coat around him, tightly fastening it around the waist. He was dressed completely in black padded leather. All the better to completely disappear in the darkness. Pulling a small, wired charge from his bag, he placed it on the kitchen door and set the timer.

Cocking his two pistols, he ducked down beside the door and waited to enter the ballroom at just the right moment.

* * * * * *

As the applause died down and Latham took his seat, the crowd of elite citizens each sat at their respective tables and began to converse on a wide variety of topics.

Suddenly there was a loud explosion. Wood, plaster and smoke exploded furiously across the room. Several people seated near the kitchen were thrown from their seats like rag dolls. Tables and chairs near the kitchen doors dispersed across the room and toppled people over as they sat clueless as to what was happening.

Screams filled the ballroom as people scurried like rats toward the exits. Pushing each other over and trampling on the fallen, they quickly realized the doors were barred from the outside and there was no escape. Panic ensued. In the confusion, Latham remained seated as he watched the chaos unfold before him.

As the smoke and debris began to settle, a lone man dressed completely in black entered through the gaping hole that used to be the kitchen door.

* * * * * *

Crossfire stepped into the ballroom with his two pistols extended at arm's length and ready to open fire. Surveying the situation, he felt it best to grab the attention of everyone in the room. Firing off two shots in the air, one from each pistol, Crossfire saw everyone stop cold in their tracks and turn to face him. As he scanned the room, he saw Robert Latham sitting calmly at the other end of the room.

"Today you all honor that man seated before you. You honor his charity and shower him with praise. I'm here to tell you all that Robert Latham has no honor and is responsible for a multitude of sins. His corruption and greed will turn this city to darkness. Be warned of who you place on a pedestal, as this man will surely line his pockets with your blood," Crossfire boomed across the room as loud as he could.

From the corner of his eye, he noticed a stocky man edging toward him. He saw that the man was ill-dressed for the occasion. No doubt a cop.

"Don't move!" the man said as he aimed his sidearm directly at Crossfire.

"You've got me, cop."

"Detective Sloan, Metro City Police," Sloan said bluntly.

The gun was directly in arms reach, so in one quick motion, Crossfire stepped in and thrust his elbow into the wrist of Sloan. The gun flew from his grasp, and before it hit the ground, Crossfire bashed his own pistol to the side of Sloan's head. Sloan crumpled from the blow and hit the floor hard with a sickening thud. Turning his attention, and his pistols, back to the unsuspecting crowd, Crossfire locked his eyes on Latham once again.

Walking toward the industrialist, Crossfire noticed a glimmer of light reflect under the table next to his enemy. He recognized tycoon Edward Truman instantly and saw he had a small firearm aimed at him as he approached the table. Without thinking, Crossfire stepped to his left just as the gun was fired. His strict military training and reflexes kicked in and before the empty shell casing discarded from Truman's gun could hit the floor, Crossfire fired off three rounds.

All three found their target. Truman slumped in his chair and fell forward onto the table. Shifting his gaze back to Latham, Crossfire saw that Truman's blood had splashed all over his left side. Latham had not even flinched. The thought of how cold his heart must be ran through Crossfire's mind. He knew then that he had made a mistake in being there, that this attack on his enemy had been too soon and that he had underestimated Latham. It would prove difficult, if not impossible, to intimidate the fiend. He felt Latham's gaze penetrate him and realized at that moment he was dealing with a monster.

He needed to retreat, to think. His plans were in disarray. His enemy was stronger than he had anticipated. He had been too rash, too bold, in his quest for vengeance. Intimidating and threatening Latham clearly wouldn't work. Stripping him of all he held dear, his wealth and power, hitting Latham close to home, struck him as perhaps a better course of action. But he needed to leave, to formulate new ideas, a new plan. This hadn't worked as he had hoped.

With the pop-hiss of a canister from his belt, Crossfire tossed the small grenade into the center of the room. Smoke billowed from the canister and it spun from the force. As the cloud filled the room, Crossfire darted back through the kitchen and out into the hallway.

As he ran down the hallway to the emergency stairwell, he realized just how mistaken he had been with his methods. The last thing he wanted was for Latham to build up a defense and be even more secretive in his illegal dealings. Reaching the stairs, Crossfire decided he would lay low from now on and strike when the time was right. In his quest for revenge, he had lost sight of what was important, of what methods worked best. Even if it took him years, he would destroy Robert Latham, and enjoy doing so. He also vowed to himself, the next time he faced his nemesis, it wouldn't be behind a mask.

He would do it face to face.

~ Chapter 9 ~

METRO CITY - PRESENT DAY

Paul sat in the Lair grasping the communicator and wondering how someone could get close enough to kidnap Max. The truth of the situation hit him hard—his identity must be known to his newfound enemy. That thought chilled him, but the danger to Max troubled him even more.

Feverishly pushing buttons and manipulating the screen on his console, he was determined to get a lock on Max's location. Eventually giving up, he swiveled in his chair to see Leena, worried and pacing the floor, throw her hands up in defeat.

"I just don't understand. After bringing me back home last night, Max said he was going to work on the Daimler in the garage and to call him if I needed anything," Leena said, her voice filled with concern.

Paul stared in disbelief as the tracking signal on Max's communicator flashed red. "Whoever this man is, he must have a vast knowledge of electronics. He's disabled Max's tracking signal."

"I'm worried, Paul. You said he was holding Max as an insurance policy? If he snatched him out of the garage, he has to know who you are."

Her face was painted with despair and panic. Reaching out, he gently grabbed her hand and tried his best to soothe and ease her worry.

"It definitely seems that way. The only thing we can do right now is try to find him and pray he's okay. We'll worry about what this man knows once we find him."

"Where do we start?" Leena asked eagerly.

"When I questioned Estalido," Paul said, "he mentioned that he and Palmer were paid to be diversions by some man they'd never seen before. That must be the man holding Max. I say we find Eddie Palmer and see what he knows. Hopefully he'll be able to shed more light on this mystery man."

Leena walked to her computer, typed in some information, grabbed a printout and handed it to Paul. "The police have an APB on Palmer, so he's probably lying low right now. He may have even left the city."

"Could be, but we have to find him either way."

Looking at Leena, Paul sighed deeply and took her hand again. "We're going to find Max, I promise. If we want to find Eddie Palmer, we need to start with Charlie Grieco," Paul outlined. "Palmer used to work for Grieco running a pawnbroker business that acted as a front for an illegal gambling operation."

Leena appeared more worried than before. She eyed Paul lovingly. He noticed her eyes begin to tear up as she stared at him.

"Assuming he knows about you...about The Wraith..." she said, "he could destroy everything."

"We need to focus on finding Max. Nothing is as important as that," Paul said calmly.

He stood and took Leena in his arms. He vowed that if any harm came to Max, he would make this new enemy pay.

Pay dearly.

*   *   *   *   *   *

Crossfire turned the coin over and over his knuckles as he sat at his workbench. It was beautiful, that much he acknowledged. Whatever reason Latham wanted it, it was not worth the lives that were lost in obtaining it. Pocketing the coin, Crossfire stood and began to pace the floor.

It didn't make sense to him. Questioning Charlie Grieco in his hospital bed offered no answers. Grieco had no idea why his boss wanted the coin, nor did he know Latham had even been searching for it. Crossfire believed Grieco and knew he was a coward at heart.

The golden coin, as he had discovered years ago, was over two thousand years old and had been sought countless times over the centuries by various parties. It was heavy for its size and beautifully decorated with what appeared to be a Roman warrior holding a spear in his left hand and a lion's mane in his right. At his feet were laurels and directly behind him, a lion seated at a throne wearing an ornate crown. On the reverse side was a large coliseum with two giant statues of the same warrior on either side of the entrance.

Crossfire had discovered the coin, and why Latham was consumed with possessing it, on his return to Karbah after escaping the hell of the Iraqi prison. The villagers had given him shelter and supplies as he planned to make his way to the border and into Kuwait. Whilst hiding in Karbah, he decided to investigate Latham's presence there years before and find the direct cause of Devil Company's demise. The villagers spoke callously of Latham and how he was completely consumed about finding the coin and sent in his own private military squad to do just that. They were forced from their homes when Latham's goons set to work in their frantic search for the coin. The Iraqi military soon caught wind of this and clashed with Latham's men. Many lives were lost in the battle that ensued.

Crossfire remembered the villagers being so hospitable toward him, despite what he had originally been hired to do—a kindness he vowed to one day repay. They seemed to truly pity him as he explained his involvement and how he was hired to originally find the coin, but was imprisoned immediately after losing his squad. As he realized the errors of what he had tried to do there, they revealed to him the legend of the coin and how they had hidden it from Latham's men, knowing his greed and lust for the coin would only bring more destruction to their village and, potentially, the world.

Crossfire knew that Devil Company shouldn't have been there to begin with and cursed the day he agreed to take on the mission. He believed that had it not been for Latham's involvement in the area, his men would still be alive today.

Grabbing the dog-tags from around his neck, memories of that fateful night in Karbah came flashing back. He swore as the memories swelled up inside. He planned to wash his hands clean with Latham's blood and put his nightmares to rest. He salivated at the thought of finally having his revenge. Revenge for Devil Company. Revenge for his imprisonment. Revenge for the innocent villagers of Karbah.

Vengeance would soon be his.

* * * * * *

Entering the interrogation room, Sloan was ready to get this over with. He had already questioned Joey "Heels" Estalido without much success and was determined to get the answers he needed.

Looking at Estalido cuffed to the small desk, Sloan grumbled as he closed the door behind him. Nodding to his partner Rosa Perez standing in the corner, he sat down and glared at Estalido.

"Okay, it's like this," Sloan said. "We want to know where your accomplices are. We want Eddie Palmer and the man that hired you both. You're going to give us what we want to know or you're going to be in for a world of hurt."

He shot a glance at Perez and noticed she looked concerned. He knew her well enough to realize she was feigning concern to help intimidate their prisoner. They often played off each other like that and it often yielded results.

"I already told you what I know. I have no idea where Eddie is. He's probably hiding out somewhere. About the guy who paid us...neither of us knew him," Estalido pleaded.

"Something tells me you know more than you're letting on. I'm going to give you to the count of three to tell me or else I'm going to ask my partner to leave the two of us alone. You won't like that, I promise."

Estalido shifted uneasily in his seat and looked away, clearly concerned at the thought of being alone with Sloan. "I told you, I don't know anything about him," Estalido pleaded again.

"You're lying! One," Sloan said.

"I don't know what you want me to say. He paid us and mapped out where we were going to walk. It was like he knew we would be busted. We didn't do anything wrong, I don't know what else to say."

"How does conspiracy to commit a terrorist act grab you? You know more than you're letting on. I think you're scared of him. Two."

"I...I...I don't know who he is, I swear it!" Estalido said desperately as he squirmed in his seat. Beads of sweat began to emerge from his receding hairline and trickled down his face.

"I don't believe you. Three," Sloan said as he leaned forward to look Estalido directly in the eyes. Narrowing his vision and not taking his sight off of Estalido, Sloan raised a hand toward Perez. "Perez...would you mind giving Mr. Estalido and myself a few minutes of privacy please?"

"Sure thing," she said as she headed toward the door.

"Oh, and unplug the camera on your way out. I'd like this to truly be a private conversation," Sloan said smiling as he continued to glare at Estalido. He cracked his knuckles slowly and methodically.

"Wait! Don't leave me alone with him. Please. I'll tell you what I know," Estalido blurted out.

Sloan smiled and winked to Perez, who took up a position in the corner of the room. His plan had worked, as it so often had in the past. Perez nodded subtly to him, indicating her understanding. Estalido sat with his head bowed, not noticing a thing.

"Well, go ahead," Sloan said, turning his attention to Estalido.

"All I know is that the guy has it out for Robert Latham," Estalido said, raising his head. "He found us through one of Latham's men, Charlie Grieco. The guy didn't say much and handed us our instructions and payment in envelopes. He said he would kill us if we didn't do what he said. After seeing how much he paid us just to walk across town, we figured it was worth the risk. He refused to give us his name and said he would contact us after the job was done."

He paused briefly before continuing. "All I can say is that he's got some crosshairs tattooed on his neck right here," Estalido said as he pointed to a spot on his neck.

"I'm done now," Sloan said as he stood up. The mention of the tattoo caused the hairs on the back of his neck to rise up. He'd seen this perp before.

"Wait! That's it?" Estalido questioned.

"Come on, back to your cell," Perez said as she uncuffed him from the desk and led him to the door.

Sloan exited first and headed straight to his desk. He remembered that tattoo Estalido described. It was several years back, before Perez had become his partner, but he remembered it well.

Rummaging through his desk, he finally found what he was searching for. He pulled a newspaper clipping from a stack of crumpled papers that was buried deep in the drawer. The headline was one he would never forget:

MASKED-MAN TERRORIZES CHARITY BENEFIT! ONE DEAD, MANY WOUNDED!

Staring at the article, he remembered the night vividly. It was a benefit dinner honoring Robert Latham when some lunatic brazenly entered and shot the place up, killing a man and yelling abuse at Latham before making his escape. Sloan had even copped a whack on the skull for his troubles.

He remembered seeing the ski-mask ride up slightly on the assailant's neck. It was the same tattoo that Estalido described.

Still staring at the newspaper clipping, Sloan didn't hear Perez walk up behind him and jumped when she spoke.

"Do you know who the mystery man is, Bob?"

Turning around to face her, he held out the clipping for her to see.

"No, but I think I know who might."

~ Chapter 10 ~

Charlie Grieco limped down the steps of the Metro City Memorial Hospital. He had been released a few moments earlier and was eager to leave and resume his duties. While he waited for the limousine to pick him up, he pulled out his cell phone and made a call. After several attempts, for no-one was answering, he decided to leave a message.

"Eddie, you know who this is. I'm coming to see you, so I want you to stay where you are. Your pal Estalido is in jail. I'm afraid he'll squeal. We need to talk, now."

Pocketing the phone, Grieco leaned on his crutch. He hated having to rely on it but there was nothing else for it.

As the limousine pulled up to meet him, the driver scrambled out and opened the door so Grieco could get in. Once in, he pulled in his crutch and sat it across from him. Grieco watched the driver hurry back to the front and slide in.

"Where to first, Mr. Grieco?" the obedient driver asked.

"I need to go to this address," Grieco replied as he leaned forward and handed the driver a slip of paper.

* * * * * *

Leena watched the limousine pull away while seated at a table outside a small deli across the street. She stood casually and walked around the corner to her small car, hopped in, and started the engine. Pushing a small button on the hidden transmitter in her ear, she heard a familiar voice.

"Leena, do you have a visual?" Paul asked.

"I do. Grieco was released from the hospital, placed a call, entered his limo, and is now headed west on Sunset Avenue. I'm keeping a safe distance back and following."

Navigating her car carefully, she watched the limousine closely.

"Okay, let me know where he ends up and then return home. The Wraith will personally check it out tonight."

"Will do. Over," Leena said as she pushed the transmitter button again.

The limousine made several turns before finally stopping at a small, rundown laundry service in a dangerous and seedy portion of the city. Leena watched from the end of the street as Grieco struggled to get out of the car and entered the building.

"Paul, I've got a location and sending it to you now. I'm on my way back," Leena said as she pushed the transmitter button and keyed the address into her cell phone. She then put the car in drive and eagerly headed home.

* * * * * *

Grieco struggled through the back door of the laundry service building. The facility was once a business that cleaned uniforms, work garments and cloth supplies that many companies across Metro City used on a daily basis. When the business began to collapse under the recent economic decline Latham Industries bought it to act as a front for a criminal safe house and illegal gambling operation, headed by Grieco and Eddie Palmer. A certain amount of laundry business was still sought and provided for there to ensure any unwanted intrusion by the police.

Looking around the run down facility as he made his way through the maze of rusty steamers and oversized laundry buggies, Grieco nodded to several workers as he limped by. The interior was shabby at best, as the steam and chemical mists from the giant machines wafted upwards through the expansive room. The tiled flooring was cracked in numerous places. Years of abuse from the daily routine of washing and treating industrial cloth had taken its toll.

Reaching a small elevator hid inconspicuously under a small set of rusted metal stairs, Grieco slid a small panel open and pushed the down button.

The elevator ride was brief and soon the doors opened revealing a large, open room with three doors leading off to various adjoining rooms. The main room was more or less a living space for those privileged enough to use it as a safe house. A broken down couch, with torn and stained grey fabric sat in front of a large television that hung crookedly on the wall beside a small window and dilapidated computer station. The faux wood paneling and cheap linoleum flooring gave off a dank smell.

Looking around, Grieco noticed the room appeared to have been recently occupied. Empty soda bottles, pizza boxes and junk food wrappers littered the floor in front of the television. He saw that the small computer was powered up as though someone had recently been using it. Feeling oddly apprehensive, Grieco began nervously looking around for any sign of life.

"Eddie?" he called out.

Receiving no answer, Grieco began looking in the adjoining rooms. The uses for the rooms varied, but normally they were used for counting money or storing a variety of items. They were wire-free and had been routinely swept for any sign of bugging or other such device, which made their illicit business easier to conduct.

Opening the first door he came to, he immediately froze in horror when he looked inside. Suspended from the ceiling by his neck was Eddie Palmer. His hands were bound behind his back and he appeared to have been the victim of a vicious beating just before being strung up. Pinned to his shirt was a folded note. Frozen in place, Grieco stared in disbelief as he watched Eddie's lifeless corpse dangle in front of him. Looking closer at the note, a chill shot up his spine as he saw his own name emblazoned on the front.

Slowly reaching forward, Grieco extracted the note as gently as he could but Eddie's body still swayed as he pulled it free from his shirt. Feeling a sense of intense dread, Grieco unfolded the note and read it. He stared at the words on the page and read them several times over. It was simple and easy to understand, but he somehow felt as though things were about to get even worse. Glancing up at Eddie, he quickly looked back at the note and read the cryptic words once again. It read:

No witnesses, Charlie. Check his pockets.

The note was signed with a symbol of crosshairs written in red. *Blood?* It was obvious to him who was responsible for this.

Why is he tormenting me? Surely it's Latham he's after? None of it made any sense.

Grieco patted Eddie's pants gently and felt a small lump in a front pocket. Reaching in, he pulled out a very small, sealed envelope. The envelope was heavy for its size and the front was adorned with red ink—*blood again?*—reading:

To Latham. A present.

Not wasting another second, Grieco pocketed the envelope. He nervously pulled out his phone, dialed a number, and waited.

"We have a problem," Grieco said uneasily a few moments later.

* * * * * *

Robert Latham stood at the large window at the rear of his office looking out on Metro City. Staring like a silent emperor, he watched as the city bustled and moved. This was *his* city and he refused to let anyone try and stop him from controlling it. Behind the scenes or not, illegally or not, Latham reveled in the fact that he had built his empire from the ground up.

Behind him, Charlie Grieco limped in on his crutch. Seeing a faint reflection of him in the window, Latham casually waved his hand for him to be seated. Grieco ignored the request.

"Eddie Palmer is dead. Crossfire..." Grieco groaned.

Turning, Latham smiled at Grieco as he sat down in his high-back chair. "Who is Eddie Palmer?" he asked as he grabbed his glass of aged Scotch and took a sip.

"An...an associate of mine. He helped me run the laundry gambling operation. This note was pinned to his body," Grieco said as he remained standing.

He handed the note to his boss, who scanned it carefully. Moments later, Latham tossed it on his desk and shrugged his shoulders.

"Is there anything more?"

"Yes. This was in his pocket," Grieco said as he produced the small envelope and handed it over.

Scanning the envelope, Latham turned it over in his hands. After a few moments, he grabbed a sharp letter-opener from his desk and sliced the envelope open. Inside was a folded piece of paper. Unfolding it, it read:

Dear Latham,

This is indeed the coin you so desperately searched for many years ago. I want you to accept it as a gift. I want you to realize that soon, I will take from you all that you hold dear and destroy you. Let this coin be a reminder that even though your quest for power may prove to be temporarily successful, ultimately you will fall. After you have lost everything, I will take the only thing you have left...

Your life.

Latham crumpled the note and tossed it across the room. Picking up the coin, he turned it over and over delicately in his hands. He had searched decades for this coin and after giving up and believing the coin had been destroyed or lost, it now lay here in his hand, delivered by his enemy. It was symbolic and upsetting all at once. Latham detested this new menace and vowed to find out who this man was and make him pay the ultimate price for his brazen insolence. Smiling wickedly at Grieco, who now sat across from him appearing bewildered and curious, Latham crossed his fingers and sat back in his chair.

"Charlie, I have a job for you."

~ Chapter 11 ~

The Wraith leapt from rooftop to rooftop in the cool night air. The moon was unusually bright and seemed to blanket Metro City in a series of eerie shadows. Moving quickly toward the small laundry service building Leena had identified, he wove in and out of the shadows like a wisp of smoke.

As he approached the ledge of the adjacent building, he checked his Christopher Ward C60 Trident watch and witnessed, from his vantage point several stories up, the last few workers leaving for the night. Making his way down the fire escape, he leapt from halfway down and landed on the thick gutter pipe snugly bolted to the brick exterior. Sliding the rest of the way down the pipe, he gracefully landed and sprung up quickly to conceal himself in the shadows between the two buildings.

Surveying the area, he saw a small basement level window that was open and big enough for him to squeeze through. Its glass was extended out on small metallic arms, so with a quick pull The Wraith wrenched it free and slipped inside.

As he hit the floor, he cautiously stayed crouched and eyed his surroundings. He had entered a large room that appeared to have been recently occupied. It certainly didn't look like a laundry on this level. Jutting off in various directions, he saw several doors that he figured were smaller adjoining rooms. The TV and computer had been left on and the floor was littered with garbage. Directly behind him, he noticed a small elevator. Surmising this was a safe-house, he eyed the computer keenly and sat down by it. Multiple windows were open on the screen containing an intriguing series of images and articles about Iraq, Robert Latham and a mysterious coin. He didn't wish to risk staying longer than he needed to, so he pulled a small flash drive from his belt and downloaded what he thought was relevant.

Once the download had been completed, he pulled the drive from the computer and placed it back in a pouch on his belt. As he stood, he detected a metallic click behind him. It was a familiar sound he had heard many times before; someone behind him had cocked a gun.

The Wraith turned slowly. There a large man stood brandishing a powerful handgun. The man looked older than perhaps he was, but he was in great shape. His muscles seemed to stretch the limits of the tight black shirt he wore. His face was scarred and appeared to have received a great deal of punishment. From this angle, The Wraith could just make out a tattoo of crosshairs on the left side of the man's neck just below the slicked back hair that met his shoulders in a tight pony tail.

"Hello, Wraith," the man said casually.

The Wraith said nothing and stared the man down. Tactics whirled in his mind. He was cornered and escape was impossible at that point. His only option was to delay his enemy and get him talking until perhaps another option became available.

"I'm glad you made it and found what I wanted you to find," the man continued.

Only a battered and broken down couch stood between them and The Wraith knew if he could get the gun from him, he would stand a fighting chance. He knew this had to be the same man who kidnapped Max as he recognized the voice. He needed to keep him talking, so he decided to see how much information he could get without a fight.

"Before the police arrive, I wanted to meet you face to face. We have a common enemy. How does that old saying go? The enemy of my enemy is my friend? Well, my friend, I had to meet the man who was also responsible for waging a war against Robert Latham."

"You called the police?"

"Of course," the man replied.

"Who are you?" The Wraith growled.

"You may call me Crossfire."

"I could call you a terrorist," The Wraith mocked.

"Hardly a terrorist," Crossfire smirked. "My actions cannot be considered a terrorist attack. I think precision strike is more fitting."

The Wraith stared at him with contempt. He knew this man was trying to take Latham down and had some sort of vendetta against him, but his methods were completely insane. And innocent lives had been caught in the middle of this madman's feud. This had to stop.

"Where's Max?" The Wraith said, changing the subject.

Crossfire paused briefly, as though searching for the right words to answer.

"I won't kill him if you just do what you're told, which is stay away and let me work."

"I don't take orders from terrorists," The Wraith growled.

"There's that word again. I'm no more a terrorist than you are. You wear your mask and cape while dancing through the shadows unseen and spreading fear in dime store hoods. I take my fight straight to the enemy, my friend," Crossfire returned.

"I'm not your friend," The Wraith said through clenched teeth. His anger was increasing and he was growing tired of the verbal back and forth. He needed to know more and needed more time to come up with a plan of action.

"How do you know who I am? How did you get close enough to get to Max?" he threw out hoping Crossfire would take the bait.

"I'm good at what I do, what I was trained to do. I've been watching Latham a long time now. I know everything about him, his associates and his enemies. That includes you, Wraith. I've been following you, watching you fight the scum of this city. Indeed, I followed you here tonight." He chuckled a little. "It took a long time, you cover your tracks well, but eventually I was able to trace you back to your base...Mr. Sanderson," he said with a mocking tone.

The Wraith felt galled at that, but said nothing.

"To show you what a sport I am," Crossfire said, "I gave you enough information to get you started on bringing Latham down your way, should I fail in taking him out in mine. But, I'm also giving you a chance here to help me. Join me and we can rid this city of Robert Latham forever."

"You kidnap my aide, kill hundreds of people and you expect my help? You're insane!"

Crossfire chuckled briefly again. "Well, I see you've made your choice then. So be it. You let me handle Latham my way and your little friend won't be hurt. If you try to track me down, I'll kill him. It's that simple," he said as he began to back toward the elevator. "Waging a war on crime is one thing, but you wouldn't like waging one against me." He pushed the elevator button.

The Wraith noticed him backing away and knew he had to do something. The sound of police sirens in the distance made Crossfire glance toward the same window The Wraith had entered just moments earlier. The glance was all The Wraith needed to spring into action.

Leaping up and over the tattered couch, The Wraith connected a hard right to Crossfire's jaw and grabbed his handgun with his left. He twisted the gun and was shocked when it didn't budge from Crossfire's grasp. The punch only caused Crossfire to stagger back a small step and The Wraith was surprised to see the villain smile back at him as if he seemed to enjoy the blow. Crossfire swung and sent a punch directly at The Wraith's mouth. The pain was intense and he knew instantly that he was dealing with a man who was an expert in hand to hand combat. The powerful strike caused him to stumble back a step before quickly regaining his defensive stance.

He saw Crossfire quickly holster his gun.

Obviously he doesn't want to kill me...yet?

Another opportunity arose and he connected two more punches, but Crossfire neither flinched or reeled from the blows. The Wraith was shocked to see how he shook them off and lunged forward at him. He realized just how massive and heavy his body was as they careened across the room and landed in a heap on the floor. Crossfire quickly pinned The Wraith's arms to the floor with his knees, then threw multiple punches at his face, smiling the entire time. The Wraith exerted himself and managed to tilt his body just enough for Crossfire to lose balance ever so slightly. That was all he needed to flip the villain to one side and he was free. Both stood quickly, re-asserting a fighting stance.

The elevator door opened just as The Wraith lunged at Crossfire, sending them both tumbling inside. Landing on top this time, The Wraith wrapped his arms around Crossfire's neck and began to squeeze. Suddenly, The Wraith was hurled upward into the air as Crossfire stood and his back struck the small metal beams of the elevator's ceiling. Despite his protective suit, he still felt the impact.

He tightened his hold on Crossfire's neck. He saw the villain's face turn several shades of red and then purple, as he continued to try and choke him into submission. Crossfire still stood and, rocking back and forth, smashed The Wraith against the elevator wall repeatedly. He was not relenting.

The trip upward didn't take long and when the doors opened up on the laundry main floor, both men spilled out. The Wraith continued to try to choke Crossfire into submission or unconsciousness, but it was no use. The man appeared to be inhuman when it came to pain.

The Wraith was again hurled into the air as Crossfire quickly stood, but his grip didn't relax for an instant. He knew he had to act quickly, as the police sirens were getting closer by the second.

He has to black out eventually, The Wraith thought.

He tightened his choke-hold even more and dug his knees into Crossfire's back. Thinking he almost had him when Crossfire dropped to one knee, gurgling for breath, The Wraith loosened his grip slightly to get a better hold. In doing so, Crossfire reacted quickly, reaching up and wrapping his immense hands around the back of The

Wraith's head. Before he could think, Crossfire had flipped him over and he landed harshly on the laundry's timber flooring. This new adversary was certainly a powerful one.

As he stood, a giant combat boot flew directly at him and struck him squarely in the face. He literally saw stars before hitting the floor hard. Darkness beckoned, but he fought the urge with all his might, and clarity of thought soon started to return to him.

Standing proved to be difficult and upon opening his eyes, he felt as if he had been hit by a train. The pain was incredible and he tasted blood on his lips.

It had only been moments but somehow Crossfire was gone, vanished without a trace. Shaking the pain from his mind, he focused on his own escape as he heard police cars squeal to a halt outside the building.

* * * * * *

Sloan sprang from the passenger side of the car the second it stopped. Perez quickly ejected from the driver seat a split second later. Both, with guns at the ready, saw a large man disappear into the shadows between the buildings.

"What's going on down there, Perez?" Sloan yelled over the sirens.

"Unit B, follow that suspect," she shouted to four officers who had just exited their own vehicles.

"Get someone to secure the building. I'm going in," Sloan said as he nodded to his partner.

"Unit A, surround the building and all available routes out! I want this area locked down now!" she ordered as she motioned for several more officers to surround the exits.

* * * * * *

As Sloan approached the building's main entrance, he saw movement in the shadows inside through a window. Grabbing the door handle, he found the door was locked. Swiftly improvising, he smashed the glass insert in the upper portion of the door with the butt of his revolver. Carefully reaching inside, he turned the bolt-lock and shouldered his way in. His gun raised, he looked around for any signs of movement.

Grabbing his flashlight, he held it under his gun and began to creep through the laundry. He was certain there was someone else in here.

"Come on out with your hands up. The building is surrounded and all exits are blocked," Sloan shouted, his voice echoing throughout the room.

Hearing what sounded like wings flapping overhead, he looked up to the above catwalk and saw a figure dart into a narrow doorway.

"Freeze!" he shouted as he made his way toward the metal staircase.

Easing up the stairs, he heard movement below. It was Perez creeping through the front door he had just shattered. Shining his light toward her to get her attention, he motioned for her to stay put as he continued onwards.

Reaching the top, he peered through the narrow door, feeling it best to stand back. Holding himself steady beside the door, he shone his light inside and cautiously peered in once again.

For a split-second he caught a glimpse of a darkened figure standing on the windowsill. Hitting the figure with the light, he saw The Wraith look back at him just before jumping out into the night. Running to the window, Sloan looked out and saw nothing but the lights of the city streets. There was no sign of The Wraith.

Feeling dejected, he slowly made his way out of the office toward the stairs. Perez met him at the bottom. Before he could tell her all that had happened, she held her hands up.

"Bob, you need to see what they found downstairs."

~ Chapter 12 ~

Max awoke with the frightening realization that he couldn't feel his arms or legs. His jaw and mouth throbbed with pain and he had a vague recollection of being punched, but his memory was fuzzy at best. His neck was stiff and hung so low his chin touched his chest. When he raised his head to get a visual of his surroundings it cracked with searing pain. Regaining his wits and looking around, he noticed he was now sitting in a chair at the opposite end of the room to where he was previously located, with his arms tied behind him and his legs bound under the chair. Securely fixed, he was in pain, but thankful he was no longer strung up like an animal. With feeling slowly returning, ever so slightly, to his limbs, he wondered just how long he had been out.

Looking around he noticed the room was no longer dark and he could see more than just the workbench he'd sighted the last time he was conscious. The room was vast and rectangular. Suspecting he was in a warehouse of some sort, he scanned the area for any indication of his exact whereabouts. In the center of the room was the workbench and just beyond it was the large hook he had been suspended from earlier. He also saw a large assortment of wooden crates and metal lock boxes that varied in size.

To his immediate right was what appeared to be a large car under a dusty drop cloth, its tires just visible underneath. From the size and shape of it, Max assumed it was probably a muscle car of sorts. His attention from the car waned and the pain became his central focus once more. He felt as if he had been in a car accident and barely survived the experience.

Closing his eyes, he tried to turn his neck to get more comfortable and relieve some of the pain in his head. Resting for a few moments, his agony subsided somewhat, but this was short lived as he opened his eyes wide when he began to hear voices coming from the workbench.

"Yes, Charlie," a man's voice said over what Max figured was a small speaker. The voice was low and he could barely make out what was being said let alone who was saying it.

"Sir, the laundry's been raided. We didn't have time to remove Palmer's body," a second voice said.

"I find this news disturbing and disappointing, Charlie," said the first man again in a voice that sounded to Max like Robert Latham.

From behind him, a door slammed shut and footsteps eased toward him. The large man who had kidnapped him had returned and walked directly past him and straight to the workbench. He sat down and Max noticed he was smiling. He began fiddling with a few switches and knobs on what appeared to be a receiver. Suddenly, the voices became louder and more distinct.

"This mess has to be cleaned up. Crossfire has to be stopped. I don't want this leading back to me."

Crossfire laughed at that and Max felt a chill run up his spine. *Crossfire? At least I now know my kidnapper's name.*

"I expect this to be cleaned up and finished, you hear me? Take care of it!"

Crossfire switched the receiver off and stood, turning to face Max. He had a look of conceited calm on his face.

"I bet you're wondering who that was, right?" he asked Max.

"Not really, to be honest," Max shot back and shifted his gaze away from his kidnapper and to the car.

From the corner of his eye, Max saw Crossfire stand and walk toward him. As he approached, he shifted directions and walked directly toward the car.

"Well, at least you now know my name," Crossfire said with a smile, echoing Max's thoughts. He grabbed the drop cloth and pulled at it. "I know you have a love for cars, so maybe you'll appreciate mine. I'm sure it will give that Daimler you work on for your boss a run for its money."

Max watched as Crossfire slowly pulled the cloth aside to reveal the car underneath.

"Do you like it?" he asked Max as he dusted his hands off.

Max said nothing. It was a beautiful car, to be sure, but in his condition he really didn't care.

"It's a 1968 V8 Mustang GT 390 Fastback."

Max merely nodded, not knowing what else to do or say.

"It's one of very few left and it took a long time to acquire," Crossfire continued. "Steve McQueen drove one in the movie *Bullitt*. His was green, which doesn't suit me. I've made a few modifications to meet my personal needs, but overall, it's the same car." He rubbed a grease-spot from the hood with his shirt.

Max didn't know what to think. First he was kidnapped, then brutalized by this mountain of a man, now he was trying to bond over a classic car? He would almost laugh at the situation if he still wasn't in so much pain.

"So...now that we're bonding, how about you let me go?" Max said with a little bravado.

Crossfire strode toward him. Leaning down, he looked Max directly in the eyes and smiled. Max noticed Crossfire's neck was red and slightly bruised as if he had recently been in a fight.

"I can't do that," the villain said. "I need you here as insurance. I have a lot of work to do and I need to be allowed to do it. Your boss knows you're alive and well...for now."

Standing back up, Crossfire left Max and went back to his car. Throwing the cloth into the air, he flapped it outward and gently covered the car back up. Max wondered how this man had encountered The Wraith and wondered if he got the neck injury from that confrontation.

"Did he do that to your neck?" Max blurted out without thinking.

"Let's just say I introduced myself, made him an offer and he refused," Crossfire said as he straightened the cover on his Mustang.

"Well, you're lucky to be talking to me now then," Max shot back, his voice tinged with sarcasm.

"I think he's the lucky one, friend."

* * * * * *

Paul removed his cowl and gently placed it on the table beside him. Gingerly, he pulled his Wraith suit down to his waist and sat there uncomfortably staring at himself in the tall mirror on the wall. His face was red, swollen and bruised. His lips were smeared with light stains of blood. Stretching his neck and side, he ached as he turned to see as much of his back as possible. A large purple and yellow bruise was starting to form there. His protective suit had taken the brunt of the punishment, but there was only so much armor one could place on one's back whereas he expected his face would be punished from time to time as the cowl left his mouth unguarded. As much as his back stung, he realized he had come away from the battle with some bumps and bruises only. Crossfire was certainly an able adversary, however, one worthy of his best efforts.

Walking into the Lair, Leena was carrying an ice pack and a few sterile cloths. Paul spun the chair around to face her. She winced slightly when she saw his face.

"It's not *that* bad, Leena," Paul said.

She said nothing as she handed him the ice pack and began to look more closely at his injuries.

"He followed me to the laundry. Asked me to join him in taking out Latham," he said. "He's intent on starting a war but I'm not sure he realizes the ramifications of his actions. As powerful an enemy as this Crossfire is, Latham is in a whole other league of malevolence."

"He's obviously very dangerous, though. What can we do about him?" Leena said, dabbing at his lip.

"I don't know, but he left me," Paul said, reaching to his belt, "this."

"A flash drive?"

"Not the drive itself, but what's on it," Paul revealed. "Load it onto the isolated system and scan it for viruses and tracking software."

"Got it," Leena said, taking the flash drive and moving over to the system in question.

Paul was very worried. The city had only recently borne witness to a deadly gang war between Latham and another crime lord, Ma Tzi. Countless had lost their lives in the process. But a potential war between Latham and Crossfire?

It didn't bare thinking of.

* * * * * *

"Careful there!" Sloan barked orders at the Metro City CSI team in the basement of the laundry. Frustrated that he had let The Wraith get away, Sloan took it all out on his team.

Officers and technicians scurried about him, but all Sloan wanted was answers. And so far, none were forthcoming.

"Taking their sweet time, Perez," Sloan said to his partner, who had just joined him. "The Wraith was here. I want to know if he's responsible for this."

"The body...it's Eddie Palmer," Perez said, ignoring his moaning.

"Yeah, I figured as much," he grunted as he watched the CSI officers continue meticulously dusting the room for prints and roping off sections of the room.

Perez came up and patted his shoulder. He knew she understood his frustration.

Before any further words could be spoken, Perez's phone rang. She took a few moments to listen, then hung up.

"That was Smith down at the precinct. Latham Industries owns this building."

"It's gotta be a front," Sloan said. "I know Latham has plenty of legitimate businesses, but this laundry? In this part of town?"

"There are some card and other gaming tables in some of the rooms downstairs," Perez revealed. "Other parts of this place look to me to be some sort of safe-house. But who killed Eddie Palmer and why?"

That was the big question that gnawed at Sloan. Still frustrated, he moved over to the elevator and pushed the button. There was nothing more he could do there until the lab boys had fully done their sweep of the area. He barged his way into the elevator when the doors finally opened. *What is The Wraith's role in all this? Did he kill Palmer?* He hated the idea of a vigilante prowling the streets of his city, but he somehow didn't think it likely. Then who? That punk with the tattoo? More likely.

But who is he? And more importantly, where is he?

As the doors closed, Sloan leaned against the wall and hung his head. This was all too much for one night and going on zero sleep the past two days, he was done and calling it a day.

~ Chapter 13 ~

Latham eyed Grieco through narrow slits as the latter limped from his office. Sitting down, the crime lord pulled the beautiful coin from his pocket and turned it over and over in his hand. It was truly unlike any coin he had ever seen. Studying it closely, he admired the detail in the soldier that, reportedly, had been completely hand-carved into it.

It was a priceless piece dating back over two-thousand years that had supposedly vanished somewhere in the Middle East—*Iraq?*—without a trace. He had spent most of his adult life secretly researching and searching for the coin and then one day it was delivered to him by a man who wanted to destroy him. The irony was not lost on him.

But why would Crossfire simply give it to me? And why in such a roundabout way? None of it made any sense.

He therefore assumed it was a fake, a joke to enrage him further. But if Crossfire expected Latham to engage in further game-playing, he had another thing coming.

Turning the coin over in his hand, Latham still felt strongly that it must be a fake, but it did look incredibly old. If it *was* a fake, it was a very good one. Opening a small glass display case in front of him on his desk, he carefully placed the coin inside on the plush felt trim.

He stared at it briefly and found himself being mesmerized by it. He blinked and shook the feeling from his mind.

This is some *fake*, he thought. *What is going on here?*

Resisting the urge to pull it from the glass case and hold it in his hands again, he grabbed the phone beside him. Punching a button on the phone without looking, he found it hard to avert his gaze from the coin. His eyes were fixed on it and his mind raced with anticipation.

"Yes, sir?" a female voice said over the phone, shaking him from his dreamlike state.

"Get me in touch with Dr. Gregory from the city gallery. I have something I need him to see."

"Yes, sir. Will that be all?"

"For now," he said as he dropped the phone on the cradle beside him and continued to stare at the coin.

* * * * * *

A giant display of the mysterious coin rotated on the large monitor in the Lair. Paul rotated the coin's image with his finger and manipulated it in order to study its fine details. He admired its beauty. It would be a prize addition to any museum or gallery in the world. It truly was something to behold. The display beeped and with a slight move of his finger, a small text-filled window popped up. Leaning forward, he began to read intently.

"Leena, listen to this," Paul said to his life partner.

Leena approached the computer and began looking over his shoulder to see his discovery.

"Legend has it the coin predates the birth of Christ," Paul said as he pointed to the screen and continued reading to her. "According to the legend, the coin was one of three given to Jesus by one of the three Magi the night of His birth. He was also given frankincense and myrrh by the other two, but the gold was apparently given in the form of three identical coins."

"That's quite a story," Leena said.

"The coins," Paul continued, "were apparently lost during the time of the Third Crusade. Until now..."

"You mean...this coin is the real thing? The legend is real?"

"Could be. That would explain why Latham wants them and why his people were in Iraq looking for them. The last known possible location for the coins was the village of Karbah in Iraq. An expedition there in the twenties attempted to find them. It ended in bloodshed and death. We're told two of the coins were destroyed in the mêlée. The remaining one was never found."

"Bloodshed and trouble seems to be the legacy of these coins," Leena said pointedly. "But why does Latham want this remaining coin so badly? Surely he wouldn't go to all this trouble for just a simple artifact to add to his collection? There has to be more to it than that."

Paul turned to face Leena. "The legend goes on to say that whomever possesses the coins will have power one can only dream of."

"But two of the three coins have supposedly been destroyed."

"I'm sure Latham must know this. I'm betting he thinks the sole remaining specimen could well impart enough power for his purposes. He's clearly been searching for whatever of them he could find."

Paul turned back to the screen and continued reading. Leena remained by his side.

"No, wait," he said excitedly a few moments later. "It says here that possessing one of the coins grants its possessor immortality. *That's* why Latham wants it. Whether it grants any sort of power or not, he wants to live forever!"

Leena gasped and clutched Paul's shoulder tightly. He knew how she must be feeling. The thought of an immortal Robert Latham exerting his power and influence forevermore truly chilled him to the bone. Such a power would potentially grant him the ability to rule all. Not just the city, but the country, even the world! He had to be stopped.

"But...it cannot be true. It has to be mere legend, ancient mythology," she said, perhaps hoping against hope.

"We don't have the luxury of knowing that. Regardless, Latham believes it to be true, and so do others, and they're no doubt willing to do anything to obtain the coin."

Paul watched Leena take it all in. He realized it was a lot of information to absorb and make sense of.

"Is there anything further?" Leena finally asked.

"A little," he said. "The coins are called *Monete Della Trinità*. In English, it translates to *Coins of the Trinity*. Three golden coins were given that night representing God, Jesus and the Holy Spirit. So says the legend."

"Perhaps we have some more information on the legend in our archives section," Leena outlined. "An old book or manuscript, possibly."

"Good idea. I'm sure the answers are here somewhere. We just have to dig further."

Sitting back in his chair, Paul caught sight of Leena gazing at him. Her beautiful blue eyes sparkled in the Lair's powerful overhead lights. It was the power of their love that kept him going and contributed to the strength he had to wage his never ending war on crime. He wondered what he'd ever do without her.

She smiled at him before turning on her heels and heading for the elevator to the upper levels and Lair exit.

* * * * * *

Sloan sat at his desk and cursed the stack of papers and files piled up there. Thumbing through the reports, he couldn't find what he needed and tossed a stack of papers in the waste basket beside him.

"I've got nothing here, Perez. Nothing. Zip. Zilch. Nada," he said as he grabbed his coffee mug.

Perez, sitting across from him, peered over the stack of files and papers in order to see him.

"It's here somewhere, Bob. Just be patient and keep looking."

"We have to find something to connect The Wraith, Eddie Palmer, Charlie Grieco and this mysterious terrorist to Robert Latham. I know there's a link somewhere. There has to be," he shot back as he sipped his piping hot coffee.

"I agree, but if we can't find a link to them all, what if we found a connection between, say, two of them and start there?" she said smiling.

"You're right. Well, we know Palmer and Grieco are linked, as Palmer worked for him at that bogus laundry. And

Grieco is Latham's right-hand man," Sloan said, almost to himself more than to his partner. "But how does this terrorist yo-yo and The Wraith factor into this?"

"Have you considered that your hatred for vigilantism has caused you to put The Wraith into something he may not be mixed up in?"

Sloan stood, shooting Perez a strong look. "What was The Wraith doing at that laundry then? He must be involved."

"He may just have been investigating the crime as we were, or somehow been given the same tip we were," she said.

Sloan shot her another look, then thought better of it and sat back down.

"We have a few options, but I think the best is to question Charlie Grieco. Remember that witness who saw him exiting the laundry prior to our discovering the body?" Perez said after a few moments.

"I agree. Let's find him and show him how Metro City's finest can play," he said grinning as he sat his coffee down.

"What do you have in mind?" she asked.

"I don't know. I'll improvise something when we get there," Sloan said smiling.

~ Chapter 14 ~

Grieco limped through the Latham Industries building toward the elevators. He still used his crutch to help him walk, but despite favoring his uninjured leg as much as possible each step seemed to cause him serious irritation. With each agonizing movement he silently cursed Crossfire.

Reaching the elevators, he pushed the down button and propped himself against the wall to relieve some of the pressure on his leg. He wondered what Crossfire's next move would be and what he could do to stop it.

The tiny bell indicated the elevator had reached his floor. He snapped from his fantasy of putting his own bullet in Crossfire and watched the elevator doors slide apart.

Shuffling toward the elevator, he saw two familiar faces, a man and a woman, exiting the elevator and glaring at him. He knew them both all too well and was not pleased to see either of them.

"Charlie Grieco," Sloan said. "We'd like to question you in regards to the murder of Eddie Palmer." He flashed his badge at Grieco.

"I don't know anything about that," Grieco replied nonchalantly. He knew they had nothing on him, save that Palmer had been killed in his building.

"You refuse?" Sloan asked, raising an eyebrow.

Grieco nodded but said nothing.

"Perez," Sloan started, a look of sadistic glee on his face, "place him in protective custody."

"Are you two completely insane? Surely this is some kind of joke," Grieco said trying to laugh off the absurdity, as he saw it, of the situation.

Moving toward him, Perez removed a pair of handcuffs from her hip and began to place them around his wrists. Irritated but not wanting to cause a scene, he made no further fuss.

"Am I under arrest?" Grieco asked.

"Now why would we do a thing like that?" Sloan responded in a sly manner.

"I hope you two have good lawyers because once I'm through with you, I'm going to make sure I own your badges," Grieco spat through gritted teeth.

"You have the right to remain silent," Sloan said. "If you give up that right, I have the right to get very nasty with you etc. etc."

"You have nothing on me," Grieco growled, struggling a little against his cuffs.

"Don't we? We have you at the crime scene hours before we discovered Palmer's body. I think that's enough for starters," Sloan said as he helped Perez load Grieco into the elevator. "C'mon, let's go down to the station."

Grieco was fuming inside, but he realized there was no use fighting it. Obviously he had to go in for questioning. He knew he wouldn't be there long and needed to keep his cool. It wouldn't do for him to lose it all at this stage.

No, that wouldn't do at all.

* * * * * *

Paul set down his newspaper as he stared at the television in his expansive living room. He watched as Charlie Grieco was escorted from Latham Industries by two familiar faces. Detectives Bob Sloan and Rosa Perez led Grieco down the front steps and into a squad car. The news-ticker on the bottom of the screen indicated that Grieco was being questioned on suspicion of murder and a press conference was to follow shortly. Paul couldn't help but wonder if this was all a ploy by his old friend and former colleague Sloan to push Latham into doing something erratic.

Before donning the mantle of The Wraith and taking over the life of Paul Sanderson, Michael Reeve was a good friend and colleague of Bob Sloan on the Metro City Police Force. He knew Sloan well and admired the man's dedication to his job. Knowing that Sloan was a man who wanted immediate results, he wondered if the detective actually had anything on Grieco, or if he was planning something bigger.

Watching intently, Paul almost didn't see his butler, Jonathan Simpson, walk up behind him. Looking back, he saw Simpson holding a cordless phone and nodding for him to take it.

"For you, sir," Simpson said as he handed the phone over and turned to walk away.

"Hello?" Paul said.

"Are you watching the news?" a familiar man's voice said after a long pause. It was Crossfire.

"Yes," Paul returned.

"Good. This was not my doing, but helps me no end. I will take Latham apart at the seams and want to remind you to keep your distance and let me work."

Paul was furious at how Crossfire seemed to have the upper hand at every point, but waited before speaking again. "Go on," he said finally. He wanted Crossfire on the line long enough for the computers in the Lair, to which the phones of Sanderson House were linked, to trace the villain's location.

"We have a common enemy. Remember that," Crossfire said bluntly. He paused slightly before continuing. "Oh, and keep watching the TV."

The phone went dead and Paul felt sure the call hadn't been long enough to trace, but he would check the computers in the Lair shortly anyway.

Paul set the phone beside him and looked back at the television. The news-ticker announced Commissioner George Harrison would be holding a press conference, on the steps of Metro Police Plaza, in around thirty minutes time. Paul felt uneasy about the warning Crossfire had given him.

What could possibly happen next?

* * * * * *

Commissioner Harrison stood on the steps of police headquarters and looked out at the sea of reporters, photographers and television cameramen. He waited briefly for the press to settle down before speaking.

"Ladies and gentlemen of the press...you have all assembled for information. Every citizen of Metro City wants to know who is responsible for the recent terrorist attack that leveled the Latham Logistics building. Today, as you all saw, we are taking a suspect into custody for questioning. We believe he isn't directly connected to the bombing, but can shed some light on the attack and possibly lead us to those responsible. I'm asking you all to show continued patience as we work around the clock in order to bring these terrorists to justice. That's all for now, I won't be taking any questions at this stage," he said as he turned to walk back up the steps behind him, with the press clamoring for more.

Without warning, a series of gunshots rang out in the vicinity. Bullets peppered the steps and walls around Harrison, sending concrete fragments into the air. The crowd, screaming and panicking, began to run in all directions, creating mass confusion. Reporters and cameramen scrambled to cover the chaos as best they could.

The gunshots continued. Harrison bounded up the steps toward a column to the side of the main entrance. Upon reaching cover, he quickly turned and raised his sidearm. Scanning the area, he saw nothing but turmoil. People were running in every direction as the bullets ripped along the ground around them.

"Everyone get off of the street!" he attempted to yell above the chaos. Seeing no one could hear him, he decided to take matters into his own hands. Raising his pistol to the ready, he charged back down the steps and into the chaos. Dodging bullet fire all around him, he moved erratically, like an agile animal being chased by a predator in the wild. He ducked and slid beside a news van and braced his back against the open door.

"Get to safety!" he screamed as he tried his best to direct the herd of people off the street while still taking cover. "Help! Get these people away!" he yelled at two officers pinned down by the gunfire beside their squad car.

The officers were only a few yards away, but in such a situation, under heavy fire and thus unable to offer any assistance, they might as well have been in a different country.

As the bullets continued raining down, Harrison suddenly realized no one appeared to have been injured. Based on the shots around him, the gunfire also appeared to be overlapping, meaning there were two shooters. Looking up to the adjacent buildings, he saw muzzle flashes coming from a small balcony across the street.

With the people scurrying to safety, Harrison used hand signals to attract the attention of the nearby officers toward the gunfire coming from the balcony. Harrison noticed it was on a higher floor looking down on the street. Knowing the building hadn't been occupied for years, he realized it was the perfect position for an ambush such as this. But why?

Glancing around again, he saw more muzzle flashes stemming from a closed underpass about a block away. Giving the officers a sharp whistle to get their attention again, this time he nodded to the underpass so they understood they were hemmed in from two directions and reinforcements from headquarters behind them were pinned down as well.

Knowing that the shooter would soon have to reload, he waited to make his move. Seeing people scramble down alleys and into buildings to avoid being shot, he was sure someone would get killed if they didn't take out the gunmen soon, despite his seeming intent to miss everyone and everything. Looking away from the news van, he saw the street had cleared except for himself and the two officers. Across the street and down the alley, a crowd of press agents were standing there filming the whole debacle. His mind raced at the stories that would grace the headlines and wondered just how much the people of Metro City could take.

They had to do something, there and then. Patting his bullet proof vest under his shirt for luck, he checked his gun and spun around the van door. Opening fire up toward the balcony, he nodded for the two officers to do the same toward the underpass. As they did so the rampaging guns seemed to concentrate their fire close to Harrison and the officers.

Out of the corner of his eye, Harrison saw one of the officers fly off of his feet and hit the ground screaming. Ducking back around the van door, he saw that the officer had taken a bullet to the shoulder, but it didn't appear fatal. The officer hit the ground, but was able to scramble back to cover and nodded to Harrison that his wound wasn't serious. As he weighed his options and surveyed the area, police sirens began to blare in the distance. Reinforcements were no doubt coming from other precincts and he had probably less than a minute to hold out.

Bullets continued bouncing off the ground all around him and the van was taking serious hits as well. Harrison looked up to see that the front of the police plaza was peppered with holes from the rampaging gunfire. Concrete dust had kicked up all around him. He looked over at his fellow officers again and saw that the fire they had been taking had ceased and it was now concentrated on his vantage point by the news van. With each impact, he felt the van rock and vibrate. He knew that whatever guns the shooters were using, the caliber was high enough to eventually rip the van to shreds.

But surely they'll run out of bullets beforehand.

Crouching behind the van and unsure of the purpose of the attack, Harrison felt his blood pressure shoot up ferociously. With a surge of anger at the situation that was so completely out of his control, he felt helpless and wondered what the public reaction would be. With lives on the line, he couldn't help but feel as if he was letting the city down, but he could do nothing more under the circumstances.

He took a few more shots at the balcony, before ducking back behind the van for cover. Suddenly, the sound of glass shattering behind him was almost instantly followed by a cacophony of gun shots. He turned to see a plethora of guns sticking out of a series of police headquarters windows, all firing at the balcony. Harrison smiled. It was time to fight back.

As the sirens grew closer, the attacking gunfire suddenly stopped from both directions. Checking his watch, Harrison knew that the whole incident had taken place in less than two minutes, but it had felt like an eternity. Peeking around the van door, he saw blue and white lights flashing rapidly from the squad cars approaching the underpass. Looking in the other direction, he saw more lights speeding toward him and realized that this wasn't going to be a day Metro City would soon forget.

~ Chapter 15 ~

Crossfire sat holding two small controllers that that connected to two monitors. Setting them down, he switched off the monitors and turned his attention to the television next to him. He saw chaos on the news as their reporters on the scene tried to capture the war that was being waged in downtown Metro City. Watching intently, he saw shaky camera footage replayed of gunfire ripping across the street in front of police headquarters. Looking over at Max, still bound to the chair and staring back at him with contempt, he smiled widely at his handiwork. Turning back to the news, he picked up the phone on the table in front of him.

* * * * * *

Robert Latham was standing in his office while watching the television, located in a buffet to the side of his desk. He couldn't believe what had just happened. His right-hand man Charlie Grieco had just been arrested and taken away for questioning, and now someone was attacking the police themselves in their very heartland. Not just someone— Crossfire! He could see that Crossfire was playing the media against him. Even the police force themselves were bound to think this attack was revenge for the arrest of his deputy.

He saw his enemy's plan played out on television for all to see. Crossfire wanted the city to turn on him and knew it was only a matter of time before that started to happen. Fuming, he jumped ever so slightly when his phone rang. He stormed to his desk and punched the speaker button.

"What?!"

"Did you like my show, Latham?" Crossfire's familiar voice rang out over the speaker.

"Listen to me you son of a—"

"No! You listen to me! You're slowly losing everything you have. How does it feel?"

"I will have your head for this!" Latham yelled and punched his desk. The impact caused the glass case holding his precious coin to jump slightly.

"No, I will have *your* head. Soon," Crossfire said ominously as he hung up the phone.

Steaming with anger and hatred, Latham swiped the contents on top of his antique desk off on the floor and then flipped it right over. Papers, folders, his phone and the glass case holding the coin went flying across his office. The anger he felt was something he'd never experienced before. He'd never been so out of control and, right now he didn't even care. Not about his losing control, not about his office, nothing. All he felt was white-hot fury.

Grabbing his office chair, he hoisted it up and tossed it effortlessly across the room, toppling and smashing several of the displayed busts of the great dictators he so admired. Down came the heads of Julius Caesar, Mao Zedong, George W. Bush and Donald Trump in turn.

Seething, sweating and panting from rage and exertion, he vowed to make Crossfire pay for this transgression.

* * * * * *

Bob Sloan approached his heroic boss. He saw the worry etched on Harrison's face and wished for a split second that he could take the man's troubles unto himself. His respect for his boss was unequaled among Metro City's finest and he felt awful for him. Terrorists were running riot in their city, attacking the police in their own building, and they had been virtually powerless to stop them. That fact galled him no end.

Sloan had a squadron of investigators and CSI officers going over the attack sites with a fine tooth comb. Ordinarily he would be there with them, urging them for results, but not this time. He had Grieco ensnared and he wanted answers. His fury was unheralded. He wanted blood. He wasn't going to let the mafia capo go without getting the answers he needed.

"Can you believe it, Sloan?" Harrison said, looking up from his seated vantage point in Metro City Police Plaza. "What on earth are we up against here?"

"I don't know," Sloan replied, starting to leave. "But I'm going to find out."

* * * * * *

"I told you already, Eddie Palmer was a former, and I mean former, business associate of mine. I haven't seen him since he was released from prison some time back," Grieco said angrily.

Sitting in the interrogation room, Grieco pulled at his arm that was cuffed to the table. His leg hurt tremendously and his rage was so intense, he felt as if he could almost breathe fire.

"I'm sorry, Mr. Grieco," Perez said, speaking in a soft, calm voice, "but witnesses have placed you at the laundry just hours before we found Palmer's body there. Further examination of the body could take several weeks. Would you like to rephrase what you just told me so we can speed this along? As a murder suspect we can hold you indefinitely. I'm sure you wouldn't like that."

"I want my lawyer present," Grieco shot back.

"Have it your way," Perez said as she stood up to walk out of the room.

As she opened the door, she walked smack-bang into her partner. He moved to speak, but Perez held up a hand.

"C'mon, let's leave him to stew a little while. We can come back later," she whispered as she closed the door behind her.

* * * * * *

Leaving the library with a stack of books, Leena noticed the traffic was horrible. She wondered if it was a sign of something ominous and inching forward slowly she knew it would take forever to get home and share her findings with Paul. At that point, her cell phone rang.

"Hello?"

"Leena, just missed you at the library. Get home as soon as you can," Paul said.

"Paul, what's going on? Traffic is terrible, much worse than usual. There's a frenzy about it all."

"There's been a shoot-out in front of Metro Police Plaza. Try to find an alternate route and avoid that area at all costs," Paul said calmly.

"A shoot-out? Let me guess, Cross—"

"Yes," Paul said bluntly.

"On my way," Leena returned as she pulled her small sedan onto the curb and slowly rode it around the line of traffic and toward a side-street.

Turning down a street she normally wouldn't take, she adjusted her route to guide her home. Following the turns closely, she navigated through a seedier part of Metro City toward the harbor. The harbor front was well out of her way, but she figured traffic would be much lighter here and she was right. She hoped the detour wouldn't delay her too long.

Driving parallel to the harbor, Leena noticed the rundown buildings and empty warehouses that filled the area. She thought back to when this part of the city bustled with jobs and prosperity not that long ago; she couldn't help but feel sad at the decline. Then it hit her that the decline had started when Robert Latham began buying up property in the area. And it was also since then the harbor had kept The Wraith busy with criminal activity.

As her mind drifted, she noticed a large black car whip out from a warehouse onto the street behind her. The vehicle was an older muscle car and was gaining on her fast. Hoping the car would just pass her, she checked her rearview and side mirrors by the second to ensure her own safety. Looking ahead, she knew that there wasn't a road to turn off for some time.

The windows in the car behind her were tinted beyond the legal level. She couldn't see the driver and the car was now so close she could hear the roar of its engine. The car crashed into her rear bumper. She slammed her foot on the gas, sending her Mini speeding ahead. Her car was faster and more durable than the typical Mini, courtesy of Max, but it wasn't any match for this brute of a car pursuing her.

What do they want? she thought, as she fought for control of her car.

After several moments of tension, the car careered out from behind to ride parallel with her into oncoming traffic. Still unable to see the driver, she began to fear for her safety and eased off the gas in an effort to shake her pursuer.

Without warning, the muscle car swerved in front of her and braked. Instinctively, Leena pressed down hard on her brakes and cut the wheel. Her car spun into the other lane of oncoming traffic and stopped sharply. Glancing up from the wheel and trembling a little, she saw her attacker's car speed up and disappear down a side street.

Looking up just in time to see an oncoming car slam directly into the passenger side of her car, Leena had no time to brace for impact. She didn't feel the pain instantly, but felt a warm and wet sensation begin to trickle down her cheek as her head slammed against the exploded airbag. Before fully realizing what had just happened, Leena's consciousness began to slip away. The last thing she remembered before everything went dark was seeing various pedestrians run toward her car.

~ Chapter 16 ~

Paul sat for several minutes and stared at a three-dimensional map of Metro City. He knew Crossfire had to be close by, but didn't know where to start. In a city the size of Metro, he could literally be anywhere.

Paul scanned his earlier phone conversation with Crossfire again on the massive computer within his Lair and tried nailing the coordinates down. He knew Leena would be home shortly and he welcomed the thought of seeing her again. He missed her when she was working, and although today was like any other work day for her, he was concerned. Metro City was reaching boiling point with Crossfire's war against Robert Latham and he hated knowing his beloved Leena was out there potentially in the thick of it. He also knew people were going to soon question the police department's ability to keep them safe.

Whoever this man Crossfire was, wherever he was, he had to be found and brought to justice.

Getting a pinpoint location was difficult, especially on such a short phone call but Paul was determined. Not only had this man waged war on Robert Latham, he had kidnapped Max, thus waging war on The Wraith as well. He'd left Metro City reeling in his wake of destruction.

Pushing the computer to its limit, Paul tried several tracing methods and finally came up with a vague location in the harbor district. Narrowing it down even further, the computer screen showed a three block radius that the call had originated from. It was better than nothing. Indeed, it was more than he had originally thought possible.

Suddenly, his butler Jonathan Simpson burst through the doors into the upper level of the Lair. His face was fraught with emotion as he leaned over the railing and faced Paul.

"I'm sorry sir, but there has been an accident," Simpson said, barely keeping his composure.

"What? What's happened?" Paul asked.

"It's Leena, sir. She's been in an accident and has been transported to Metro City Memorial Hospital."

"Is she...is she okay?" Paul sputtered.

"I don't know, sir."

Nothing else was said as Paul bolted from the Lair and took off into the house.

* * * * * *

The balcony was littered with hundreds of spent shell casings. Sloan stepped over them to where a mounted machine gun was nestled against the steel railing overlooking the street below. Connected to the gun was a camera and what appeared to be a remote control receiving antenna.

"Well, well. What have we got here?" Sloan asked the nearest CSI officer.

"This attack was done by remote control. There was no one ever here."

Looking around the scene, Sloan was impressed at the set-up. Whoever had rigged the machinegun had known what they were doing and had access to, and the money to afford, the very best of equipment.

It's that whacko with the tattoo. It has to be.

"Genius..." he said to himself as he continued to survey the scene.

Looking closely, he could see the remote was hardwired into the trigger and the gun had been mounted on a tripod that was bolted into the concrete flooring. The gun was belt-fed, which Sloan noticed still had bullets in it ready to be fired. The belt feed came from a metal ammunition box that was the size of a mini-refrigerator. At a guess, he figured that there was close to four-hundred rounds fired and close to the same amount ready to be fed into the gun.

Sloan pushed his way past the adjacent CSI officer and into the apartment without saying another word. Upon reaching the exit, he turned back to get another look at the apartment. Nothing. The place was completely empty and other than the gear on the balcony, there was nothing around. No signs anyone had ever been there, no clues left behind.

"Find out who owns this building!" Sloan yelled to the closest officer as he turned to leave.

* * * * * *

Paul burst through the door of the hospital room. Stopping as soon as he entered, he saw Leena lying peacefully asleep in the bed. A nurse stood beside her checking a monitor and jumped a little at his sudden presence.

"How is she?" Paul asked.

"She's fine. A bit of whiplash, but other than that, she's going to be all right. We'll keep her here for observation for a day or so, but she's very lucky," the nurse said as she motioned for Paul to keep his voice down. "She's sleeping now. We gave her something for the pain."

"Thank you," Paul said smiling at the good news.

Carefully sitting down beside Leena, he watched as the nurse nodded at him on her way out the door. He grabbed Leena's hand gently and kissed it, clutching it close to his chest as he watched her sleep. Wondering what had happened, and knowing he had only spoken to her a few short minutes before her accident, he was thankful she was going to be fine. He couldn't bear to think of a life without her.

As he sat beside her holding her hand, he felt her stir and begin to waken. Looking up, he saw she was struggling to open her eyes. He patted her hand gently and smiled. Leaning in, he kissed her softly on the forehead and sat back down. She opened her eyes slightly and smiled back at him. He saw the joy on her face at seeing him but then she moved to speak.

"...black mustang...harbor..." she managed to utter before drifting back to sleep.

Without hesitation, Paul pushed the nurse button beside her bed. Within seconds, the nurse stormed into the room and gave him a scathing look.

"Sorry, but where was her accident?" Paul asked politely.

The nurse gave him an annoyed look but quickly acquiesced. "Let me look..." She grabbed Leena's chart and began flipping through it. "It says here Sierra Drive. Isn't that down in the old harbor district?"

"Yes, it is. Thank you," Paul said as he rushed past her out of the room.

* * * * * *

Still seething with anger, Robert Latham almost didn't hear the door to his office open. His secretary stood timidly in the doorway with a tall older man following close behind her. He was well-dressed with thinning hair and a grin that would make the Cheshire Cat green with envy.

"What is it?" Latham boomed.

"Sir, Dr. Gregory is here. You requested for him to..." she started nervously.

"I know what I requested," he said waving a dismissive hand at her.

Controlling his anger, he beckoned for Gregory to take a seat before him.

"Mr. Latham, a pleasure as always," Gregory said as he extended his hand.

Bartholomew Gregory had been installed by Latham as the Curator of the Metro City Gallery as a condition of him bailing it out of financial trouble two years prior. Gregory was an expert on ancient artifacts and antiquities and his expertise was thus well suited not only to Latham's interest in the arts, which was well renowned, but also to his quest for power through any means available to him be that mythological, mystical or spiritual. If there was any truth to such legends, Latham wanted to know about it and Gregory was the man to ask in such circumstances.

"This is why I called you over," Latham said as he reached down to the floor and removed the coin from its casing. He handed it to Gregory and watched the doctor examine it closely.

There was a lengthy silence as Gregory studied the coin under his jeweler's microscope.

"Ah... Monete Della Trinità. Amazing," Gregory exhaled as he eyed the coin carefully.

"Yes. It's real then?" Latham asked, anticipation building up inside him.

"This coin was supposed to have been destroyed. If I'm correct, and the legend is accurate, this is the last one of three."

"So, it's real? Authentic?" Latham asked eagerly.

"Where in heaven's name did you get it?" Gregory probed, ignoring Latham's desperate pleas.

"What does that matter? Is it the real thing? Is it one of the Coins of the Trinity?"

"Yes. Yes, I believe it is," Gregory said finally. He rattled the coin in his hand which disturbed Latham somewhat. "But there's something wrong with it. It's lighter than it should be."

"What do you mean?" Latham enquired as he felt his blood-pressure begin to rise.

"This coin, Mr. Latham, has been tampered with," Gregory said as he gently pointed to the edge of the coin. "This is definitely one of the Coins of the Trinity, but someone has altered it."

Latham stood and began pacing. He knew it had been too good to be true. That this powerful new enemy wouldn't simply gift him that which he'd always wanted. But what was Crossfire's ultimate aim with this? Humiliation of course, but what else?

"Mr. Latham, I think you should see this," Gregory said behind him.

Stopping, he turned to face the doctor and felt his stomach bottom out as he saw Gregory holding a piece of the coin in each hand.

"It's been hollowed out, sir. All I did was gently twist it in my hands and it came apart like I had unscrewed it."

The realization hit Latham hard. Somehow, someway, Crossfire had acquired one of the previously thought of destroyed coins, or portions of it, and had contrived this *pseudo-coin* to tempt him, to hurt him. To lure him into a trap?

"What is this?" Gregory asked upon closer inspection of the coin.

Latham watched as Gregory pulled a small, black electrical device from the inside of the coin. The doctor held it up. Latham swiped it from Gregory's hand. Turning the device over in his hands, he realized immediately what Crossfire had done.

"This, doctor, is a transmitter. A microphone. A bug," Latham said through clenched teeth.

He had been tricked. Like a school boy, he had overlooked everything with the thought that maybe, just maybe, immortality was already his. He inwardly cursed his lack of thought, his lack of judgment. Crossfire had exposed a weakness within him and that both infuriated and disgusted him at the same time. He squeezed the transmitter between his fingers. It shattered and fizzed as he dropped it to the floor.

"Sir, what do you want to do with this?" Gregory asked, holding the two pieces of the coin aloft.

"Keep it. Consider it a donation to the gallery," Latham said forlornly.

He turned and strolled to the window. He peered down to the street below. A crowd was building up; most likely reporters flocking for a statement regarding the attack on police headquarters. He knew he had to either issue a statement or make an appearance in front of the cameras himself. His reputation in the city mattered to him. It was *his* city, after all. He owned it to do with it as he wished. No one would sully his name in *his* city. No one!

The phone rang, shaking Latham from his thoughts. He knew this time who would be on the other end.

No more games, he thought. *This ends now.*

"I found your surprise," Latham said as he answered the phone.

"Of course you did. It was only a matter of time. I'm just shocked it took you so long," Crossfire shot back in a mocking tone.

"You're dead. Plain and simple. The games are over," Latham spat.

"You're wrong. The games are only just beginning."

"You're dead!" Latham said again, this time shouting.

"I'm coming for you, Latham. I hope you're ready." Crossfire laughed and hung up suddenly.

Latham slammed the receiver back into its cradle, shattering the entire phone in the process. He closed his eyes, took a deep breath and then turned to face Gregory.

"I'm sorry, Mr. Latham. I have to do this," Gregory said as he raised a revolver at him and pulled the hammer back with his thumb.

~ Chapter 17 ~

Paul stood in the Lair staring reflectively at the array of Wraith costumes before him. Seeing Leena's skintight outfit brought back countless memories of her extensive training with him and how she had finally joined him as his partner. Knowing Leena was fine was all that mattered to him but now he had other obligations to uphold. His mind suddenly flashed to Crossfire and he knew that unless he stopped this menace, the people of his city would continue to suffer. The war on Latham that Crossfire was waging had now hit home and it was time he stopped it dead in its tracks. Assuming that Crossfire was hiding out in the harbor district where Leena was detouring home, it was just a matter of tracking him down.

Selecting his suit, Paul began methodically getting dressed for his nightly patrol. First the suit itself went on, then the boots, gauntlets and belt. Lastly, he placed the cowl on his head and adjusted it to fit just right. The Wraith was now ready for battle. He would stop Crossfire once and for all. Mentally preparing for what could possibly happen, his thoughts raced with anticipation of finally bringing Crossfire to justice.-Before he could do that, he needed to find out as much information about the villain as possible.

Sitting at his computer system, The Wraith decided to begin with Latham's dealings in Iraq. Knowing that had to be where the key to Crossfire's identity lay and where he believed this personal vendetta started, he booted up the files he got from the laundry computer and started his research. He knew it wouldn't be long before they again met face to face and he had to know everything he could in order to take Crossfire down.

* * * * * *

Detective Bob Sloan opened the interrogation room door and saw his suspect sitting calmly handcuffed to the table. He knew he couldn't hold Charlie Grieco any longer; the judicial system would tear him apart if he did. Sloan hadn't gotten any vital information out of Grieco, and other than a former business relationship, knew that his connection to Eddie Palmer couldn't lead to a conviction. Other than being seen at the scene of the crime, there was no evidence Grieco had been responsible for the crime.

"Okay, Grieco. You're free to go," Sloan said as he walked across the room.

"You're going to suffer for this. Mark my words. I'll have your job for this, Sloan!" Grieco threatened.

"We'll see about that one. We both know you're not telling me something, so when I find out exactly what that something is, I'll make sure that prison seems like a vacation."

Eyeing him for a sarcastic response, Sloan was shocked that the anticipated comeback never came, and instead, Grieco sat silent and glared menacingly back. Unlocking the handcuffs, Sloan watched as Grieco rubbed his wrists.

"Go on. Get out of here," Sloan said as Grieco stood to face him with another murderous glare.

"We're not through, Sloan. It would be in your best interest to forget about me. Drop your investigation now while you can still go home to your wife," Grieco slyly remarked as he pointed toward Sloan's wedding band.

"Watch that leg," Sloan sarcastically shot out.

Standing and watching Grieco limp to his freedom, Sloan was hit with a revelation. As Grieco slid by him and made his way into the hallway, he stopped the young capo short by darting around in front of him.

"One last question, Charlie."

"Sorry detective, but I'm a free man and have answered enough of your questions," Grieco huffed.

"You never told me how you hurt your leg."

He saw Grieco's demeanor immediately change. Knowing now he was truly hiding something, he edged in closer, almost touching noses, and stared him directly in the eyes.

"So, would you mind telling me how a gunshot wound was kept from police? Hospitals are required to report all gunshot wounds to us for investigation. How did you get that by us?" he asked, smiling widely.

"I think our conversation is officially over," Grieco said as he pushed his way past Sloan and continued limping down the hallway.

Watching Grieco carefully, Sloan knew there had to be a major disruption going on in the Latham empire. *But what can it be?*

As Grieco rounded a corner and disappeared from sight, Sloan pulled his phone from his jacket and made a call.

"Perez. He's on his way out now. Follow him, don't let him out of your sight. In fact, get as many officers on him as you can. I have a feeling he's going to lead us right to the answers we need."

* * * * * *

The gunshot rang out, Gregory firing but Latham didn't flinch. His facial expression didn't change in the slightest. Inside, though, he was fuming. Crossfire had, again, fooled him, gotten to him in the innermost reaches of his empire by using a close associate to attempt an assassination. Fortunately it had only been with blanks; obviously another attempt to scare him, not kill him, or not yet at any rate. But he didn't scare very easily, despite Crossfire appearing to have the upper hand at every turn.

"How did he get to you, doctor?" Latham asked casually as he turned and walked toward a bookcase stretching the entire length of his office wall.

"He...said he'd...kill my family if I didn't do as he said," Gregory stammered, his gun arm shaking intensely. "He...he also...promised me the actual coin."

"Did he now? Well, as you can see, the coin wasn't as promised was it?" Latham grabbed a bottle of Scotch from a shelf on the bookcase and began pouring himself a glass. "No matter...would you care for a glass, doctor?"

"No...no thank you," Gregory said, lowering his gun.

Looking at the reflection of Gregory in the bottle of Scotch, Latham saw the doctor lower his gun in defeat. Gregory slumped into a chair and made for a pathetic sight indeed. The gallery curator had been threatened, it was true, but he still needed to be taught a lesson. Nobody threatened Latham and lived to tell about it.

Still watching the doctor's reflection in the swirling liquid, Latham reached behind a nearby book and pulled out a small handgun secreted there.

"I'm sorry it has to be this way but you've left me no other choice," Latham said as he turned to face Gregory. "I can't have you attempt to kill me and let you walk out of here, can I?"

Gregory's face dropped with fear. The shock was visible as Latham saw the man begin to panic and shake wildly. He didn't have time to react before Latham fired.

The gunshot wasn't as loud as the revolver but it was still enough to reverberate off the walls of the office. The smell of burnt gunpowder skimmed across Latham's nose. It was a familiar smell that he loved and it brought back memories of times long gone, when he was a young man only just beginning to build his vast empire.

He watched as Bartholomew Gregory fell forward from his chair and his revolver skidded across the floor. Blood poured from the wound in Gregory's thigh.

"That was a warning, doctor. Never, and I mean never, think that you can ever threaten me again," Latham said callously as he walked toward the doctor.

Gregory lay writhing in agony holding his thigh. Latham had purposely given him a non-fatal warning shot in hopes of teaching him a valuable lesson in loyalty.

"Let us understand one thing," Latham said as he hovered over Gregory. He enjoyed causing pain and exerting his immense power over others. "You work for me and me alone. You fear me above all others. Understood?"

"Yes...yes, of course," Gregory said through clenched teeth.

Latham raised himself upright while continuing to watch Gregory writhe in pain. Raising his gun, he viciously slammed the butt of it into Gregory's head, sending him to sleep. Latham walked back to his bookcase for another sip of Scotch. As he began pouring another glass, his office door burst wide open.

"Sir, is everything okay?" His secretary looked at the scene before her in horror.

"Just fine," Latham said as he turned to her and raised his glass of Scotch in acknowledgment. "Please call an ambulance for Dr. Gregory here. He seems to have had an accident."

"Yes, sir," she said as she turned and bolted from the office.

Latham leaned against the bookcase and grinned as he took a sip of Scotch. Even though his empire had been infiltrated once again, and a close confidant had been (briefly) turned, he still felt he had won this battle. He had discovered and destroyed Crossfire's listening device and he had shown all those who defy him the errors of their ways. Yes, he had won the battle.

Now he had to win the war.

* * * * * *

Angrily, Crossfire slammed his fist into his workbench. He had feigned awareness and expectation of Latham's discovery of his listening device, but in truth, the loss of the device annoyed him. Underestimating the vile crime lord again had cost him his upper hand and now he was forced to push his plan into action sooner than originally anticipated. It wouldn't matter. The final steps to his plan were already near at hand. He had wanted just a little more time to tie up a few loose ends and really make Latham suffer, but if he had to act sooner, so be it.

Looking across the room and thinking of how his plan had been altered, he caught sight of Max looking at him. His prisoner shifted his gaze away as if not to provoke Crossfire further.

"Do you have something you'd like to say to me?" Crossfire said as he strode toward Max.

"No, nothing at all."

The lights suddenly cut off completely stopping Crossfire dead in his tracks. Immediately, a red beacon light flashed above them.

"What's going on?" Max asked.

"We have company," Crossfire said as he ran back across the spacious room to his workbench.

He grabbed a cloth covering two monitors and slung it aside. Switching them on, he picked up a small controller and began studying the monitors intently. Moving the controller around, he manipulated the outside security cameras as the display on the monitors moved and showed the perimeter of the warehouse. Crossfire froze as he brought an image into focus.

"I don't believe it! Son of a—" was all Crossfire could get out before the explosion hit and sent him reeling from his chair.

* * * * * *

Max, still tied to his chair, tipped over and crashed to the floor. The chair cracked under the force of his fall and he was able to slip free from the wood. Seizing the moment, Max used the slack in the ropes to ease his legs free. Lying on his side, he took advantage of the splintered chair and, grabbing a chunk of the chair leg with his feet, began to rub against the rope binding his hands behind his back.

* * * * * *

The explosion blew the steel warehouse door clean off its hinges and sent it flying into a stack of nearby crates. The frame and wall holding the door in place shredded and melted beyond repair from the heat of the blast.

Smoke wisped all around as The Wraith moved to the edge and peered inside the fiery doorway. Stepping over debris and burning metal, he carefully entered the darkness inside the building. The red warning light blinked eerily and illuminated his surrounds, casting strange scarlet shadows about him. Ready for anything, The Wraith stood just inside the newly warped entrance looking around for any sign of Max or Crossfire.

* * * * * *

Crawling across the floor back to his workbench, Crossfire saw the menacing, shadowy figure lurking in the doorway through the intermittent red flashes the light gave off. Reeling at how his perfect plans had been so quickly unraveled, he desperately pushed forward to save some aspect of his scheme and exact his revenge. Reaching under the workbench, he opened a small metal box that was bolted securely underneath. Flipping a switch inside, a deafening, shrill siren began to sound. Crouching, he slid his arm between two nearby crates and pulled out a large duffel bag. He quickly checked its contents and slung it across his shoulder. With his back against the table, he pulled an extremely large handgun, his favorite customized Smith & Wesson 4506-1 .45 ACP, from a drawer and stood quickly.

Scanning the room with his gun, he came to rest it in the direction of the blasted doorway.

"You've got thirty seconds to get your friend out of here, Wraith!" he shouted over the siren.

Firing off two shots blindly in the direction The Wraith last stood, Crossfire made a break for it and began sprinting toward his car.

* * * * * *

The Wraith checked the area carefully, as Crossfire's shots ricocheted past him. He needed to be on his guard.

Searching for Max, he saw a shadow struggling on the ground a few yards away.

"Max, are you okay?" The Wraith shouted over the alarm as he watched Crossfire reach his car out of the corner of his eye.

"Yeah, I'm fine, Chief. Almost free. Go get him," Max cried as he struggled to cut the final threads loose on his bindings with the jagged wood.

"Not without you. We have to hurry, the fire is spreading fast."

Without further thought, The Wraith leapt into the fray, grabbed Max up in his powerful arms and sprinted toward Crossfire's car.

The lights on the car flashed on and the engine fired up. The Wraith and Max were almost there, but he could tell Crossfire was about to put the pedal down and speed away. Letting Max down, he judged his distance in the blink of an eye, leapt toward the muscle car and hoped his calculations were accurate.

* * * * * *

Crossfire slammed the gear shift into first and released the clutch. He stomped on the gas pedal and the powerful car lurched forward and threw him back in the seat. With only ten yards available to gain speed, he pushed the gas pedal down as far as it would go and watched his RPM gauge shoot into the red.

Speeding toward the small metal loading door close to the gaping hole The Wraith had just made, he felt something slam onto the roof directly above him. Glancing out of the corner of his eye, he saw the gloved hand of The Wraith hanging on just above his window frame. Within seconds, the car struck the metal garage door and sent it hurling into the air. Glancing up in his rear-view mirror, Crossfire saw the door bounce violently off the ground behind him as he sped from the warehouse and out onto the street.

Now free from the confines of the warehouse, Crossfire was able to gain speed rapidly. He noticed The Wraith was still attached to the roof and knew he had to deal with the Dread Avenger once and for all. His base of operations had been compromised and his plans were potentially in ruin. The Wraith had to be dealt with, there and then. His first priority, though, was to get as far from the warehouse as possible before continuing his mission.

A loud boom drowned out the sound of his customized engine and caused him to jerk the steering wheel slightly. Looking again in his rear-view, he saw fire shoot straight into the sky followed by a pillar of thick, black smoke from what had been his home for the last few years. He regretted it, but under the circumstances, it was necessary. For his plans to still come to fruition, he had to destroy any evidence that could potentially be used to stop him. Nothing could stand in the way of his quest for vengeance.

He instantly blamed The Wraith for his current predicament Hatred for his new enemy welled up inside him.

I warned him to stay away, to let me work, Crossfire thought.

But his warning had gone unheeded. So be it. Now The Wraith would suffer the consequences before he moved in on Robert Latham.

* * * * * *

Reaching the Daimler parked across the street, Max was knocked off his feet when the warehouse exploded, cleansing all evidence of Crossfire and his existence in Metro. Regaining his footing, he turned back to see the building had become a raging inferno, spewing flames uncontrollably into the air and lighting up the entire waterfront. In no time it started to collapse and he could see burning debris scatter throughout the harbor. Max knew he had to leave the area immediately. The authorities would be soon on the scene.

Slipping inside the Daimler, Max felt suddenly at home. Switching on the tracking system and transmitter, the display highlighted The Wraith's location. They were speeding away from the scene fast. Revving up the engine, Max slammed the car into drive and took off after them.

"Chief, I've got you on the tracking link-up. I'm on your tail," he said as he put the transmitter into his ear.

"Good to have you back, Max," The Wraith shot back.

"Aye, Chief, it's good to be back," Max said smiling.

~ Chapter 18 ~

Detective Sloan walked to his car across the dimly lit police parking garage. He had just received several reports stating that Charlie Grieco had slipped out of sight. He felt more tired than he had in a long time. Desperately trying to connect Grieco to Palmer's death or the terrorist attacks, Sloan felt Grieco was more than likely crawling back to his boss for protection or lying low at some secret location to avoid the police. Sloan hoped it would merely be a matter of time before Grieco slipped up. When Grieco did, he vowed to be there to take him down.

Opening his car door, he was overwhelmed by the activity on his police scanner. It was if it had exploded with voices.

"...twenty-one, in pursuit," the voice said loudly as sirens blared in the background.

"Stay on that car, twenty-one. We're dispatching other officers in that vicinity for assistance," an eager voice said that Sloan recognized as the dispatch operator.

Curiosity overwhelmed him and his mind raced with possibilities. Grabbing the radio, he clicked the talk button as he sat in the driver seat and started his car.

"Dispatch, this is Detective Sloan. Can I get an incident location?"

"Sloan," the operator said in reply. "We've had an explosion in the harbor district and are currently directing units toward a fleeing vehicle traveling at high speed from the area."

"I'm en route to the area," Sloan said as he slammed the door. He didn't know why, but he had a gut feeling this was the lead he had been looking for. He wasn't about to let it slip away now. Seconds later he was speeding from the garage and out into the busy city traffic.

Picking up his cell phone, he tried his best to maintain a steady acceleration and place a call at the same time.

"Perez!" he blurted. "Don't ask me how or why but I think this waterfront business could be related to our case."

Listening intently for her reply, the color washed from his face as he heard what had happened in the short time it had taken him to walk from his office to the parking garage.

"You hit the harbor and keep things under control. I'm going after that car. Keep me informed of anything," Sloan said as he hung up and tossed the phone in the passenger seat. Turning up his police radio, he trod heavily on the gas and pushed his car to its limits. He had to catch up to that car.

* * * * * *

Looking ahead, Max could barely see the tail-end of the Mustang race through the streets. The black car swerved in and out of traffic at such a high speed, Max had trouble keeping up and maintaining the safety for other drivers on the road. He saw The Wraith swaying on the roof as he maintained his grip on the car.

Trailing further behind, Max worried he wouldn't be able to catch up and help. When police cars joined the chase, Max felt it best to retreat and try a different approach.

"Chief, it's getting too thick back here. I'm losing my visual on you and police are appearing everywhere. I'm going to detour and see if I can't somehow parallel your position."

Max waited an eternity for a reply but it never came. Constantly shifting his eyes back and forth from the road to the tracking link-up, Max knew that The Wraith was still okay but it was time to put his own plan into motion.

"I know you can hear me, so I'm taking my turn off now and will be following you on the link-up," Max said as he whipped the Daimler up a side street and sped away from the chase.

* * * * * *

The force of the wind was incredible. Unsure of the speed they were traveling, The Wraith did his best to grip the roof of the sleek Mustang as Crossfire carelessly maneuvered his way in and out of traffic. He knew Crossfire was trying to shake him loose and it was only a matter of time before he succeeded. But he also knew he had to stop the villain at all costs and minimize the collateral damage in the process so he gripped the roof as tight as he could.

Cars flew by him, sounding like tiny, buzzing insects in the wind. The Wraith found it difficult to raise his head because the wind felt as if it were repeatedly punching him in the face. The sounds of police sirens behind him grew louder and his mind flashed to the possibilities of what could happen if Crossfire grew desperate for escape. The intensity of the situation was building and he knew it was time to act.

Waiting until the right moment when Crossfire swerved around another car, he relinquished his grip on the roof with his right hand and used the wind and momentum to his advantage to sling his body completely around. Battling against the wind's force, he narrowly escaped flying backwards and rolling off the speeding car. Forcing himself forward with great exertion, he flipped onto the hood of the car instead and gripped the wipers tightly in each hand. Looking up, he could see Crossfire glaring back at him through the tinted glass. He had only seconds to act or all might be lost.

Crossfire started jerking the car left and right to try and knock The Wraith free but his grip was solid and wouldn't be broken so easily. He felt his cape whip up over his head and flap violently as they sped forward. Holding as tightly as he could with his left hand, The Wraith delivered a hard right directly to the windshield. He felt intense pain shoot through his hand and up his arm as his knuckles bounced off the bullet-proof glass. He wondered if he'd broken his hand or wrist.

Thinking quickly, he pulled a small circular device from his belt with his free, and throbbing, hand. The Wraith clicked a button on it and watched as it lit up with a tiny blinking red light. He momentarily held it in front of the glass to show Crossfire before shoving the device between the hood and windshield. He quickly flipped and turned his back to the glass, leaned up against it and faced forward. The wind was blinding and he felt his cape tug viciously at his shoulders and neck as it flapped across the roof of the car. Looking for his opportunity, The Wraith watched through squinted eyes for anything he could use as a means for escape.

* * * * * *

Cursing at The Wraith, Crossfire pushed the gas pedal to the floor and felt it slightly bend under the weight of his foot. Blinded by the body of his enemy spread across his windshield, he was reduced to using his GPS for navigation. He wondered what The Wraith had shoved under his hood, but knew it had to be something that could potentially stop him dead in his tracks. Looking down at his gauges, he saw he was doing almost one hundred and thirty miles per hour and steadily gaining speed. The RPM gauge was red-lining and the engine roar cut out any other sound. It was time to act.

The straightaway he was soaring down was nearing an end and about to merge onto a freeway that circled the outside of Metro City. Checking his speed, he knew it was time to rid himself of The Wraith once and for all.

Lifting his foot from the gas pedal, Crossfire simultaneously stomped the brake and held the wheel as firm as he could. Lurching forward into the seatbelt, he felt it pull tight before his body suddenly slammed into the seat. Hearing what sounded like a giant barrel bounce off of the hood, Crossfire looked up to see The Wraith was gone. His Mustang had stopped almost sideways in the middle of the street, and upon looking around, all he saw were cars stopping all around him. The Wraith had vanished.

Grabbing his weapons first, he then snatched up his bag, slung it across his shoulders, kicked the door open, and jumped out with two giant handguns at the ready. Scanning the area he saw people jump from their cars and take off running away from him. The street was dark except for the abandoned cars—which the owners had left with the lights still on—and the occasional street lamp. The area felt desolate but Crossfire knew The Wraith had to be close by.

The sound of police sirens grew closer and he knew they would be on him soon. He had only seconds to get away so he could still fulfill his plan of revenge on Latham. Guns raised, he carefully stepped from his car and backed away slowly as he scanned the area for The Wraith.

He looked all around his car but was surprised to see nothing there. Checking for only a brief moment, he wondered where his nemesis could have gone. Giving up and deciding it was time to go, he turned to quickly leave. As he did so, he was faced with two giant yellow glowing Eyes coming toward him out of the darkness.

* * * * * *

The Wraith knew he had the upper hand. Darkness was his ally and Crossfire had underestimated him greatly. The Eyes of Judgment on his chest grew bright and illuminated Crossfire's face from the shadows. He could see the man squint from the glow and knew it was time to finish this.

Crossfire didn't have a chance to react as The Wraith quickly lunged forward, grabbing him by the head and forcing his face to gaze into the Eyes. The sound of Crossfire's pistols bouncing off of the pavement rang out loudly and cut through the silence between them. He felt Crossfire's body go loose and he tightened his grip to compensate the effort it took to hold him up.

"Feel the pain you've caused this city. Feel the wrongs you've forced upon your victims. Feel the suffering left in your wake of destruction cast back unto you," The Wraith moaned.

Crossfire made no sound as his body went completely limp and slipped from The Wraith's grip. The Wraith watched as Crossfire's body bounced off of the ground in front of him. Something felt wrong and he couldn't figure out just what that something was. Within seconds, he clearly understood.

* * * * * *

The light from the Eyes was unexpectedly blinding, but it gave Crossfire a moment to think and plan his escape. Confusion was what he wanted and he saw, by The Wraith's expression, that he had achieved that. He had to act fast. Crossfire had studied The Wraith over time and knew his powers. He had resolved to not succumb to them if they ever met. He felt that sheer willpower would enable him to block any attack on his mind. It was that same willpower that kept him from giving up hope of escape while in the Iraqi prison. He realized that would only work during the initial stages of the Judgment Stare, for his research indicated all eventually succumbed to The Wraith's thrall. But if he could hold out initially, then perhaps there was an avenue of escape. Now was such an opportunity.

It was time to strike and with the police sirens inching closer, that time was now. In a lightning fast move, he broke free from The Wraith's loose hold, grabbed the forty-five that lay beside him, flipped his body around and aimed directly at The Wraith.

"Goodbye, Wraith," he said as he squinted to see his target through the yellow spots floating across his eyes.

He squeezed the trigger three times, quickly, and saw The Wraith fling his cape around him before he flew back off his feet and landed in a heap beside the Mustang. The Wraith crumpled and lay motionless.

Rubbing the sting from his eyes, Crossfire stood and walked toward his car.

One enemy down, another to go.

Looking down, he saw The Wraith's cape was covering most of his upper body. Kicking the cape upward with his foot, he saw The Wraith was still breathing. Turning him over with his heel, Crossfire was surprised to see The Wraith appeared virtually unharmed. There was no sign of injury or even bullet marks on The Wraith's suit.

The cape is obviously bullet-proof, Crossfire thought. *Amazing...*

"What did you put in my car, Wraith?" Crossfire asked as he aimed his customized pistol directly at The Wraith's head. He flicked a tiny switch by his thumb and a tiny red dot appeared on the center of The Wraith's head. "Your cape may be bullet-proof but your face isn't."

"...bomb," The Wraith coughed, clearly winded.

"I don't think it worked."

"You stopped the car..." The Wraith spat out as he gasped for air.

"It's such a shame I have to do this, but you've left me no other choice," Crossfire said as he cocked his gun and stared down at The Wraith. He had originally thought—*hoped*—for The Wraith's compliance, if not actual help, in his war on Robert Latham, but when that was not forthcoming he knew the Dread Avenger had to be dealt with or his plans for vengeance against the crime lord would come to a crashing halt. Nothing could stop him from wreaking terrible revenge upon the man whom most of Metro City revered as a philanthropist and hero instead of the evil murderer he was.

"Drop your weapon!" a voice shouted from behind him.

Turning his head slightly, Crossfire saw a strangely familiar man aiming a revolver and a badge at him. *How did he manage to sneak up on me?*

"You...I remember you," Crossfire said as he recognized the man as the detective who had tried to stop him years earlier at Latham's charity benefit.

"I said drop it!" Detective Sloan said as he slid his badge into his pocket and gripped his gun with both hands.

"Well, if you say so," Crossfire said as he cocked his head even more and gave Sloan a slight nod.

"Drop it now!"

With his left hand concealed, Crossfire drew a second pistol and opened fire. Sloan quickly ducked behind a nearby car for safety.

Relentlessly firing his pistols into the car and holding Sloan at bay, Crossfire suddenly remembered The Wraith. Glancing back, he saw that The Wraith had disappeared completely. Again.

This idiot cop distracted me long enough for The Wraith to get away, he thought, frustrated.

Furious, he edged his way closer to Sloan. If he had to take a cop out as well, so be it.

Suddenly, a powerful explosion sent Crossfire crashing to the ground. Quickly regaining his bearings, he looked up and saw his car was a mass of flames and rendered metal. He couldn't believe it. The sight of his destroyed Mustang sent him over the edge. Anger shot through his veins and he promptly stood just in time to see The Wraith walk into the light holding a small detonator.

Raising both pistols at The Wraith, he felt the nape of his neck heat up with a newfound hatred. He could feel his breath form into short bursts. Anger consumed him and the vague respect he once had for The Wraith was instantly erased.

"Enough of this madness," The Wraith said as he walked beside the burning Mustang.

"You're going to die here, Wraith!" Crossfire shot back as he steadied the little red dot between The Wraith's eyes.

"I know all about you, Crossfire. Or should I say Captain Jackson Thomas."

Crossfire felt white-hot at the mention of his true name. He knew what The Wraith was trying to do but he had to focus, not let his concentration waver even for an instant. Hearing that name, however, brought back memories that he had difficulty suppressing. He hadn't heard it in a very long time, and as far as he was concerned, Captain Thomas had died along with his comrades in Devil Company. He had spent years erasing all ties to who he once was. Captain Thomas was no more and the mere mention of that name sent his mind to places he no longer cared to go. He chided himself for his weakness. All that mattered was The Wraith had to die.

"That man is dead. And so are you," Crossfire said as he pulled the trigger.

~ Chapter 19 ~

Detective Perez stood in complete disbelief. The burning warehouse had been totally obliterated in the blast and she watched as fire and rescue teams scattered to put the fire out. She decided not to get too close, as she could feel the heat even from several hundred feet back. The intensity of the blaze was even too much for the firemen who stood back and blasted the remains of the building with their hoses. Only a few sections of wall and a crumpled roof remained.

Assuming that the blast was most likely connected to the Latham Logistics bombing, Perez tried to piece the puzzle together in her mind as she watched the devastation before her. Inspiration suddenly hit as she saw part of the remaining roof cave in and the firefighters jump back.

Pulling out her cell phone, she pushed the buttons and waited for a response.

"I need all available information on this burning warehouse. Send everything you have on this location to my phone immediately. Thanks."

Hanging up, she watched as Metro City's best worked hard to contain the raging inferno.

* * * * * *

Sloan woke to the sound of fire crackling. He did not remember how he'd ended up lying face down on the pavement but slowly began to mull over what had just happened. His sidearm lay in sight a few inches from his face. Picking it up, he craned his neck to see his surroundings. Pain shot through his face and head as he moved but he felt alive and relatively unhurt, which was all he cared about at that moment.

Pulling himself up on one knee, Sloan looked around and saw a sea of abandoned cars lining the street in all directions but nothing else. Holding his pistol firmly, he braced his back against the car directly behind him and pushed himself up. Still seeing no sign of anyone around, he turned to look behind him and was sure he was dreaming.

Standing several feet away was The Wraith beside a burning muscle car. Directly in front of him, with his back turned, was the terrorist aiming two pistols at The Wraith. He couldn't hear what was being said, exactly, but he caught the name Crossfire and saw the deadly intent on The Wraith's face. Someone was about to get seriously hurt. It was at that instant that Sloan remembered everything; the car chase, the battle of the two costumed warriors, and now...

Without warning, Crossfire fired his pistol at The Wraith. Startled by the shot, Sloan drew his weapon and eased around the side of the car.

* * * * * *

The bullet whizzed directly by his head as The Wraith instinctively shifted his body at the last second. He had seen Crossfire's finger twitch slightly and knew he was about to shoot. He moved just in time to hear the bullet zip by him and strike a parked car behind him.

Stepping toward Crossfire, The Wraith extended his hands in a friendly gesture. "Why don't you just hand me your weapons and no one else will get hurt." He tried to anticipate Crossfire's next move.

"Latham is the one I want. Get out of my way and I promise you no one else has to die," Crossfire quickly returned, holding his ground.

"I can't let you do that, Captain."

"Stop calling me that! That soldier died a long time ago."

"No, he didn't. I'm seeing that same man standing directly in front of me now. End this before it's too late," The Wraith pleaded.

The Wraith hoped his tactics would work. If he could confuse Crossfire just long enough to...

Sloan appeared in the background and raised a gun toward Crossfire.

"Don't!" The Wraith yelled as he saw Sloan narrow his eyes to take the shot.

* * * * * *

The shot rang out but Crossfire couldn't immediately tell where it had come from. He felt his shoulder lurch forward but he still stood strong. He saw The Wraith standing a few feet from him but he knew The Wraith never used guns of any sort. Feeling a sudden and painful burning sensation erupt in his shoulder, Crossfire knew he had been hit. Pain coursed through his shoulder into his back and neck. He managed to turn and saw his assailant. It was the policeman he had pinned down moments before, Detective Sloan, who he had forgotten about during his battle with The Wraith. He saw a tiny wisp of smoke wafting from the cop's barrel. Hatred coursed through his veins and intense pain caused his mind to drift back, back to...

* * * * * *

The memories came flooding in. He was back in Iraq, back in prison. The blows hit with each breath he took. Non-stop fists smashed into his face one after the other. He could no longer see, his eyes had swollen shut, the coppery taste of blood filled his mouth and his face was going numb from the pain. The last thing he remembered seeing was the two guards taking turns laughing and striking him for no reason. They hadn't even spoken to him directly and although he couldn't understand them, they appeared to be both mocking him and enjoying torturing him at the same time.

When they finally took him back to his cell, it was almost a week before the swelling went down and he could see again. He was used to the pain by then, used to the punishment inflicted upon him, but it was the lack of respect they displayed that fueled his hatred. He vowed to himself to escape and kill them all, one by one if he had to.

* * * * * *

As the wound throbbed and pulsated with each heartbeat, Crossfire slowly came back to the present. The horrors and pain of his imprisonment threatened to overwhelm him. He would make Sloan pay for his actions.

Ignoring the pain, Crossfire turned his back on The Wraith and fired mercilessly at Sloan. Nothing would stop him from achieving his goals.

Nothing and nobody.

* * * * * *

Sloan heard the glass of the car explode all around him. The car shook violently as he slid back down the side and struck the pavement. He had been hit, but didn't know if by glass or by bullet or how badly he was wounded. His body hurt all over and the only thoughts he had were of his wife. He didn't want to die in the line of duty. He didn't want to die on the ground.

Not here, not like this.

* * * * * *

The Wraith leaped into action and grabbed Crossfire by his ponytail. Jerking the villain's head back almost to meet his shoulder blades, The Wraith delivered an elbow directly to Crossfire's nose, breaking it instantly. The gunfire ceased as Crossfire fell helplessly to the ground. Blood began to trickle from Crossfire's nose and stream down his cheeks.

With Crossfire out of action, The Wraith sprung into the air and landed on the trunk of the car Sloan had slipped behind. Looking down at the fallen officer, he saw Sloan was still alive but had been shot and needed immediate medical attention.

"Max! Officer down! Call it in and relay our location to them," he said as he clicked the transmitter in his cowl.

The Wraith stared at Sloan. As far as he could see, Sloan had only been hit in the arm and shoulder. He was bleeding, but his wounds didn't appear fatal. The Wraith looked on with compassion as he watched his former friend and colleague slip in and out of consciousness.

Police cars suddenly appeared from everywhere, with officers pouring from their cars ready for action. They had finally made it and were making up for lost time. As the sirens whirled all around him, The Wraith took that as his cue to exit.

Assuming Sloan was going to be fine, he turned and made a run for it. As he did so, he noticed Crossfire had gone. All that remained of the menace were empty bullet casings littering the street and a burnt out Mustang.

"Max, I need your location," he said as he clicked the transmitter again.

"Two blocks north on Taylor Street. I'll meet you there."

Sprinting away from the scene, The Wraith took a moment to turn and survey the damage on the street. Cars littered the area and police milled about, though none gave chase. He knew it was going to be a long time before Metro City forgot about Crossfire. He just hoped he could stop him before he was able to get to Latham and cause untold more harm and chaos.

It was shaping up to be a very long night.

~ Chapter 20 ~

Charlie Grieco had his instructions and after spending several hours losing his police tail, he was finally ready to set the plan into motion. His instructions were clear and his resolve was solid; tonight, Crossfire died.

Walking across the construction site, Grieco inspected the area closely. It was almost completely dark, save for a few lights that had been set up around the perimeter to deter late night thievery, and he liked it that way. The site was the future home of another division of Latham Industries and thus far sat alone on the edge of Metro City in the new Metro Industrial Park complex. Owned by Robert Latham, the park was the first of many business ventures that would ensure the financial future of the legitimate side of Latham's empire. Although ground had been broken less than a month previous, construction was moving along at an impressive pace. Three levels of structural framework, two office trailers and an array of building equipment all sat nestled safely inside a high, chain link fence adorned with razor wire. Latham Industries was expanding at a stunning, rapid rate and would soon rival Sony or Apple as a global player in their field.

As he paced the muddy lot, mentally reviewing his instructions, Grieco saw the plan of action unfold in his mind and couldn't wait until it was time. Pulling his phone out of his pocket, Grieco dialed and waited for an answer.

"Sir, everything is ready," he said.

He closed his phone and walked toward the nearest office trailer.

*   *   *   *   *   *

The Daimler sped away into the heart of Metro City and mixed in easily with the regular night traffic.

"Sloan's been shot, Chief?" Max enquired as he guided the Daimler cautiously through the streets.

"Yes," The Wraith said from the backseat.

"Is he going to be all right?"

"I believe so. His wounds appear to be minor."

"What now?" Max asked as he looked into the rear view mirror and saw The Wraith staring ahead. He was focused and ready for battle.

"We have to find Crossfire before he can hurt anyone else. He has to be stopped."

"Where do we start?"

"Robert Latham," The Wraith said coldly.

*   *   *   *   *   *

Latham strode across the parking garage at Latham Industries with three armed escorts surrounding him. Walking toward his limousine, he checked the area carefully before getting inside. Making sure their boss was safe, the three escorts entered immediately behind him. The limousine instantly sped away, leaving the garage empty.

"C'mon, you filth," Latham whispered to himself as the car edged into the slight city traffic. "I know you're out there, Crossfire; watching me. You want me? You have to follow me to get me. Come and get your just desserts."

* * * * * *

Crossfire observed carefully as the limousine exited the garage and drove directly past him. Hiding behind a small retaining wall that ran parallel with the garage, he had been able to see Latham and his guards pile into the limousine. As the luxury car proceeded up the street, Crossfire aimed a small gun-like device at the back of the vehicle. Pulling the trigger, a small pop sounded followed by a hiss of gas as a small, circular projectile ejected from the device and landed on the rear bumper of the limousine.

Putting the device away, Crossfire pulled a tiny battery-operated monitor from his bag. Switching it on, a GPS-like readout appeared and he saw a tiny blue dot moving away from his location.

As he watched the blue dot move further away into the city, Crossfire touched his shoulder and felt the pain surge back. He cursed his carelessness in allowing himself to be taken by surprise so easily. He hadn't realized how affected he still was by his experiences in Iraq, but resolved to never allow himself to be compromised like that again. He could tell the bullet was lodged near his shoulder blade, but all thoughts of having it removed were pushed aside. If he was careful, his plans might still come to fruition.

Leaping over the retaining wall, Crossfire darted across the parking garage toward a small guard office beside the elevators. Knowing full well from his research that Latham had night watchmen patrolling the building instead of guards stationed, Crossfire figured he could make quick use of the office and be on his way before anyone knew he was there.

Upon reaching the office, he found it to be locked. It was simple enough to pick, but it took time and he didn't want to be exposed any longer than he had to be. Slamming his good shoulder against the door, he was able to cleanly separate the lock from the door frame and was inside in seconds.

Even using his good shoulder, the pain in the other increased. He quickly realized the bullet had to come out. Crouching down, he pulled a small, black pouch from his bag. Unzipping it, he removed tweezers, needle and thread before checking his surroundings for anything else that might be of use. Under a desk, he found a small refrigerator. Upon opening it, he pulled out a few bottles of water.

Leaning against the door for leverage, he shoved the pouch in his mouth, bit down hard and carefully inserted the tweezers into the bullet hole in his shoulder. It was an awkward position as he could barely see what he was doing, but leaning his left side against the door for support helped somewhat. He dug around with the tweezers and almost lost consciousness when he struck the bullet and forced it against his shoulder blade. He bit down hard as immense pain shot through his body. Tears streamed from his eyes as he dug around in his back, desperately trying to grab hold of the bullet.

After what felt like an eternity, but was in reality only a few minutes, he was able to maneuver the tweezers enough to grab hold of the bullet and pull it free. Relief washed over him as he held the bullet aloft. Looking it over, he saw the crumpled lead that struck his back and felt even angrier than before.

Within minutes, the wound was sewn and he was gently washing it off with the cool water. After loading his weapons and readying himself for Latham's demise, Crossfire meticulously packed his bag and slung it over his good shoulder. Standing up, he looked around the garage for any sign of the guards before taking off outside and disappearing into the darkness of Metro City.

* * * * * *

Max sat inside the Daimler, patiently watching Latham Industries. Moments earlier, he had let The Wraith out in a nearby darkened alley before parking in viewing distance of the building.

"I've got nothing, Chief," Max said into his radio.

Waiting for a response, he pulled a pair of binoculars out of the console and began scanning the area for a closer view.

"Keep your eyes on that building. I feel certain Crossfire will show," The Wraith said over the radio.

Searching the area with his binoculars, Max suddenly saw movement near the parking garage on the side of the building. The shadows seemed to come alive as he squinted into the darkness. Adjusting his eyes, he saw a glimpse of someone—*Crossfire?*—dart over a small wall and take off into a nearby alleyway.

"Chief, I've got a visual. He's heading your way," Max said as he tossed the binoculars aside.

"I saw him too, Max. Keep me on the link-up and stay close behind. I'm going to follow him from above."

* * * * * *

Crossfire felt the sudden sensation of someone following him. Like a silent stalker in the darkness, he knew it could only be one person; The Wraith.

Having just left the Latham Industries building, he took off down a nearby alley and tried to remain in the darkness as best he could. Relying on his years of military training and experience, Crossfire knew that if someone *was* following him, he had one of two options: confront them or lose them. With his plan of attack on Latham unraveling at the seams, he felt it best to weigh his options carefully before deciding the best course of action.

Checking his monitor, he saw that Latham had come to a complete stop in an unmarked area close by. Assuming this was a new area of development that had yet to be downloaded into his mapping system, he knew he had to act fast in case Latham moved again. He couldn't chase his prey all over the city on foot and stealing a car was too risky, so he had to do what came naturally. Black ops.

Before he could make another move on his true prey, Crossfire was certain he would have to eliminate The Wraith first in order to complete his mission. Knowing what he had to do, Crossfire stuck to the shadows and darted down the alley.

* * * * * *

The Wraith, perched out of sight high above the alley across from Latham Industries, saw Crossfire disappear into the shadows below. Judging by the villain's behavior, The Wraith assumed Crossfire knew he was being followed and wondered what his next move would be. Scanning the area, he saw no trace of Crossfire exiting the alley and wondered if he had disappeared into a building or the sewer system.

"What's going on, Chief?" Max askd over the radio. "Do you have a visual?"

"Keep your eyes open, Max. I'm dropping down to find him."

"Be careful," Max returned.

* * * * * *

Robert Latham walked toward the office trailer and saw Charlie Grieco slowly limping his way over. Looking around at the construction site, Latham was very pleased with the progress that had been made so far.

"Sir, all our men are in place. We're ready," Grieco said as he stopped next to his boss.

"Very good, Charlie. How many were you able to round up?" Latham asked as he looked around and admired his own handiwork.

"Eight. We have one at each corner on the perimeter, two up high with rifles and two by the trailers. We're covered, sir."

"Eight? Are you kidding me?" Latham said as he stepped closer to Grieco.

"Sir, I sent the rest to your home in case Crossfire showed there. I thought you would want your wife protected in case —"

"He's going to show here! He's out there somewhere. Watching. He'll come, I know it."

"With your three, that's eleven and I'm thinking that should suffice," Grieco continued.

"I can count, Charlie," Latham said, exasperated. "These are my personal bodyguards and I'll instruct them as to when they join the fray! We're here to make sure we remove this thorn from my side and squash him like the bug he is."

"Understood," Grieco sighed.

"Be sure to let me know when you catch sight of him. I'll be in my car," Latham said with a dismissive wave.

Latham watched Grieco limp away toward the office building. He made sure he was out of sight first, then turned toward his limousine.

* * * * * *

Having parked as close to the scene as she could, Perez moved as fast as possible, running through the abandoned cars. Weaving in and out, she was determined to make it to Sloan before he could be carted away.

Upon arriving, Perez was stunned to see a smoldering car and bullet casings littering the ground amongst a morass of broken glass and debris. It looked like Sloan had been in the middle of a warzone and she hoped for the best as she made her way to the ambulance.

Perez silently hoped her partner's injuries were minor, but her years on the force told her to brace herself for the worst. Reaching the ambulance, Perez was glad to see Sloan awake and lying on a gurney, being prepped for a trip to the hospital. Rushing to his side, she was surprised to see he was in good spirits considering what he must have gone through.

"Bob! Thank God you're okay," Perez said as she looked him over from head to toe.

"I wouldn't say okay, but I'm alive," Sloan said as he let out a half-hearted chuckle.

"It's nice to see your sense of humor wasn't shot," she returned.

"Funny. Look, I don't know where that madman went, but I could have sworn I heard him mention Robert Latham. You gotta look into that, Perez. You gotta," Sloan said as the medical response team lifted him into the ambulance.

The doors closed and relief washed over Perez. Within seconds, the ambulance sped away, leaving her standing in the street. She watched a squad of officers scurrying about investigating the scene of the crime and moving the abandoned cars off the road. Perez headed back to her car, determined to see justice served.

* * * * * *

Scanning the dark and dreary alley, The Wraith saw nothing but windswept trash and puddles of foul smelling liquid. The brooding darkness kept him on guard. He wondered if Crossfire had somehow managed to escape him. Pushing such thoughts from his mind, he crept down the alley. There was no sign of life anywhere.

Rounding the corner at the end of the alley, the buildings jutted off to the right and led toward a series of narrow alleys surrounded by rundown apartments and slender avenues covering several city blocks. Keeping his guard up, The Wraith slowly eased down toward the labyrinth of dwellings.

As the alley simultaneously opened up to his left and right, The Wraith searched the area for any sign of Crossfire. The area was dead and dark; no sign of the villain could be seen anywhere. Pondering his next move, The Wraith saw what appeared to be a manhole cover slightly ajar several yards ahead.

Making his way toward it, The Wraith was prepared for anything. Eyeing the area for anything else out of the ordinary, The Wraith crouched to lift the covering to peer inside. Instantly, he heard noises.

Movement?

Yes, underground was where Crossfire had vanished.

The sound of steel heavily scraping against concrete filled the night as The Wraith lifted the manhole cover and slid it to one side. Looking down into the sewer entrance, The Wraith saw nothing but darkness. The light of the moon helped dimly light the alley, but it did nothing for the sewer below.

Reaching into his belt for a light, The Wraith was suddenly caught off guard when he was hit across the back of the head with a hard object. Falling forward and almost into the manhole, he met the cold pavement with a sickening thud. His head pounded with each heartbeat and it felt as if his hearing and vision had been short-circuited. Turning over, he saw Crossfire standing above him, holding a metal pipe.

"Sorry, Wraith, but I can't let this continue," Crossfire said as he raised the pipe.

~ Chapter 21 ~

Max knew something was wrong. It had been several minutes since there was any word from The Wraith. With Crossfire disappearing and his boss going down to street level for a closer look, Max had a gut feeling that something just wasn't right.

"Chief, is everything okay?" he asked, flipping on the transmitter.

Minutes crept by and there was still no answer. Grabbing his binoculars, he scanned the area for a glimpse of anyone. Nothing. No sign of The Wraith, or anyone else for that matter. Moments later, Max saw a car slow down and pull into the parking garage at Latham Industries.

Who could that be? he thought.

* * * * * *

Pulling her car into the garage, Perez saw no one around. The parking area was completely empty. No guards, no cars, no one.

Strange, she thought. *There should at least be guards around.*

She exited her car and headed toward the elevators, hoping they were still active at this late hour. If Latham was here, he'd be working late in his office. Suddenly, she heard a loud noise echoing from the alley outside. Straining to hear more, Perez drew her gun and crept cautiously toward the garage exit.

* * * * * *

Crossfire swung again but The Wraith rolled out of the way, causing the pipe to strike the pavement inches from his head. Tiny sparks shot up and chunks of pavement flew upward. Crossfire quickly tried again, this time connecting across The Wraith's back.

The Wraith groaned in pain. Crossfire knew the last blow had hurt him. Edging in closer, he swung twice more and connected across The Wraith's back both times. The Wraith lay silent and barely moved.

Even with that protective suit of his, that had to hurt.

Raising the pipe again, Crossfire aimed for The Wraith's head in order to finish the hero off once and for all.

"Goodbye, Wraith," Crossfire said as he raised the iron pipe high and sized up his target.

A loud, thunderous boom echoed through the alley and the pipe went flying from his hands. Pain coursed through his hands and shot up his arms as he wondered what had just happened. Looking around, he saw nothing initially until, directly in front of him, a woman holding a gun aimed straight at him emerged from the shadows.

* * * * * *

On many occasions, Sloan had told Perez she was a great shot and it was only now that she was relieved her partner had been right. While those thoughts rattled around in her brain, she had the terrorist in her sights.

"Freeze!" she said as she stepped into the light of an overhead lamp post.

He didn't move a muscle but seemed perplexed at seeing her come out of nowhere. Staring down the terrorist who had shot her partner, Perez knew she had to remain vigilant and be prepared for anything. This man was dangerous, a killer, and she knew to fire without question if she had to.

"Now, lie down on the ground and put your hands in front of you where I can see them," Perez commanded as she edged a little closer.

The man didn't move, but instead stared a hole straight through her.

"I said get down on the ground, NOW!"

Again, he didn't move, he just continued staring her down as she took another step forward.

"You won't shoot me," he said calmly.

Holding her aim steady, she stopped easing forward and narrowed her eyes.

"Don't count on it," she said, maintaining her composure. "I repeat, lie down and put your hands out in front of you. Don't make me repeat myself again," she instructed firmly.

The man raised his hands in apparent surrender, but nothing more. Eyeing the man intently, Perez broke her concentration when she saw The Wraith stirring. In that instant, the man stepped forward and dropped into the open manhole. As he descended, she saw that his belt scraped the opening and dislodged a small device, which bounced off the ground directly beside The Wraith. Cursing her sloppiness, she rushed forward and peered down into the sewer. There was no sight of him.

"Darn it," she said.

She immediately turned her attention back to The Wraith, who was struggling to get to his feet. Holstering her gun, she put her shoulder under his arm and helped him up.

"Are you okay?" she asked as she stepped away to give him room.

"I'm fine, thanks," The Wraith returned.

She watched as The Wraith moved over to the manhole and peered inside.

"He tricked me. There was obviously someone else down there. Just my luck," he said under his breath as he picked up the device Crossfire had dropped.

"What?"

"Never mind."

"Are you going after him?" Perez asked.

"No," he said looking back at her.

"What's that?" she asked, pointing to the device.

"A way to find him," The Wraith said as he switched it on and saw the tiny monitor light up and show what appeared to be a map.

"You can't have that, it's evidence," Perez said, holding her hand out for the device.

The Wraith ignored her and placed the device into his belt.

Resigned to not getting the device, she said, "Is he the one responsible for—?"

"Yes."

"What now?" Perez asked as she backed away from him.

Knowing he was a vigilante and her partner was relentlessly seeking his capture, she couldn't help but feel a little guilty about talking with him like this; though, at this point, they had a common enemy. She had never been as against him as her partner, favoring Commissioner Harrison's begrudging support of the vigilante.

"I'll find him. Stop him," The Wraith said pointedly.

"Who is this guy? What does he want?" she asked, hoping he would agree to supply the answers.

"He calls himself Crossfire. He's after Robert Latham for reasons I don't have time to divulge."

Perez took a moment to think. She stared at The Wraith, wondering what the next move would be.

"While I'm not entirely convinced of your actions in this city, I can't deny the good you've done so far. God knows Metro needs something more than us cops have been able to provide. Go. Get after him. I never saw you and we never had this conversation."

The Wraith nodded in understanding as she turned back toward Latham Industries. Walking back through the alley, she hoped that her decision was the right one. She vowed that whatever happened, she would never speak a word about this to anyone. Not even her partner.

* * * * * *

The Wraith slid into the Daimler, causing Max to jump. Flicking the dropped cigarette from his lap, Max was relieved to see The Wraith in the rearview mirror.

"Are you okay, Chief?" Max said as he caught his breath.

"This is where he's going. So are we," The Wraith said as he handed a small monitor over the seat to Max.

Taking the small portable GPS-sized device, Max looked it over and saw a vague map with a tiny, blue dot off to the side.

"Is that where Latham is?"

"I believe so. Either way, Crossfire has to be headed there," The Wraith said.

"Where did you get this?" Max asked as he started the car.

"He dropped it in the alley."

Putting the car in gear, Max sat the small monitor on the dashboard and pulled out onto the street. As he drove, he noticed the small map turn and shift toward the blue dot.

"It looks like we're heading for the new industrial park," Max said.

He looked in his rearview for a reply that never came. Max saw that The Wraith was focused and determined to bring Crossfire to justice and wasn't in the mood for talk.

"We'll be there in a few minutes, Chief."

* * * * * *

Trudging through the sewer, Crossfire cursed the female cop who got in his way. He had dropped his monitor in his escape and knew either now had a hold of it. He had to exit the sewers quickly, as he had no way of knowing where to go underground without his tracking device. The Metro City sewer network was worse than a maze and he needed to get topside and reach Latham before the crime lord had time to move from where he had last been.

Reaching a manhole cover above him, Crossfire climbed the rusty ladder, pushed it open and slid it aside. Climbing out, he found himself in a compact and dead-end alley he quickly recognized as being only a few blocks from Latham Industries.

Nobody followed me, he thought. *Good.*

Looking around the area, he realized he was only about a mile from the industrial park. Knowing the need for urgency, he checked his weapons and took off down the alley.

* * * * * *

The construction site was quiet.

Too quiet, Grieco thought.

He stared out the window of the office trailer and surveyed the area. Seeing the guards positioned, he felt somewhat assured that things would be okay. Then again, knowing Crossfire...

Looking around, he saw the limousine where his boss was sitting comfortably, waiting for a report of any activity. Knowing that Latham was ready to end Crossfire once and for all, Grieco couldn't help but wonder if he would show. Crossfire seemed to revel in embarrassing Latham and not showing would enrage the man to no end. Especially if he was correct in assuming their enemy would target Latham at home.

Walking to a nearby desk, Grieco poured himself a cup of coffee and sat down. Looking at the security monitor that showed the outside perimeter in four little squares, he decided to sit and wait patiently.

* * * * * *

The guard never saw it coming. Turning his attention toward a helicopter crossing overhead, Crossfire was able to step in and snap his neck before he even knew anyone was there. Dragging the body away from the perimeter of the site and into a nearby ditch, Crossfire clung to the shadows and slowly made his way to the next visible guard.

Having spotted two guards positioned high up on the building's structural beams and four more surrounding the outside at every corner, Crossfire knew he had many more guards to go through to get to Latham. It didn't matter. He would gladly take down anyone who tried to stop him.

He silently worked his way through the shadows toward the next guard like a ghost and waited patiently behind a bulldozer for the perfect time to strike. Pulling a small, flat blade from his boot, Crossfire turned it around in his hand and tightened his grip. Raising his hand to aim, he slung the blade and watched as it stuck directly in the guard's neck. Springing around the bulldozer, he leaped on top of the guard and pushed the blade further into his windpipe. Grabbing the corpse by the feet, he dragged the man out of sight behind the bulldozer and into the darkness.

Moving stealthily through the night toward the next guard, Crossfire looked up to see a security camera slowly panning back and forth. Figuring his element of surprise was about to run its course if he didn't act quickly, he stopped and grabbed another blade from his boot. Sizing up the distance, he threw the weapon and saw it make direct contact, burying itself in the lens with a series of sparks.

Crossfire hoped nobody heard that. Quickly and silently, he made his way toward the next guard in hopes of dispatching him swiftly and moving one step closer to his real prey.

* * * * * *

Grieco set his coffee down and jumped when one of the squares on the security monitor blacked out. Looking closely at the other three squares, he only saw two guards at their posts. In that same moment, Grieco suddenly saw Crossfire emerge from the darkness and pull a guard into it.

Reaching for the phone, he refused to take his eyes off the monitor. Glancing down for only a second to dial the phone, Grieco looked back at the monitor to see the fourth guard was now missing.

"Sir, he's here," Grieco said with some urgency as he hung up the phone.

Standing up, he drew his gun and walked toward the office window. Seeing the guards still stationed up high gave him a small sense of relief. The relief immediately left him as he heard a muffled gunshot and saw one of the guards fall, lifeless, from their vantage point and land almost directly in front of him. Straining to see in the low light, Grieco made out a tiny bullet hole on the guard's head. He was no doubt dead before he hit the ground.

Readying his weapon, Grieco strained his eyes for any indication of Crossfire's position. Another muffled gunshot rang out, causing him to jump again. The shot sounded as if it came from a different direction this time. Looking up just in time to see the body fall, Grieco followed the second guard's descent down and watched him bounce off the ground in front of him.

Grieco darted back inside to the monitor. Before he could see anything there, a nearby explosion rocked the office and sent him tumbling to the floor. The trailer walls burst apart and sent debris crashing on top of him. Moments of calm followed and he hacked the dust and dirt from his mouth and lungs. He was pinned down but alive. From his vantage point, he saw Crossfire step through the opening in the trailer and into the light.

~ Chapter 22 ~

Robert Latham flinched when he saw the explosion. The fence and office trailer next to Grieco's position blew apart and sent debris flying across the construction site. Not taking his eyes off the blast area, Latham watched as Crossfire emerged from the darkness. He had shown his face and now it was time to put his plan into motion and remove this threat for all time.

Looking to his three personal bodyguards, Latham held up his hand and signaled for them to wait.

"Not yet," Latham said as he watched Crossfire dart behind Grieco's trailer. "Let's see what he's up to first."

* * * * * *

"Did you hear that?" Max asked as they entered the industrial park.

"Crossfire hasn't wasted any time," The Wraith returned.

"What's the plan, Chief?"

"Stop the car here," The Wraith instructed.

Max immediately pulled the Daimler into a small alcove. Before the car could come to a complete stop, The Wraith leaped from the backseat and disappeared into the darkness.

Knowing The Wraith would contact him if he needed anything, Max grabbed his binoculars and settled in. Looking ahead at the dimly-lit construction sight, he had a bad feeling things were about to heat up.

* * * * * *

Crossfire looked around the trailer and saw Grieco buried under a mound of debris. The explosive C-4 charge he had set on the fence not only tore through it like a hot knife through butter, it also blew the side of the trailer wide open.

Crossfire shoved the office desk and portions of wall off of Grieco, grabbed him and pulled him to his feet. Struggling to stand, Grieco started to slip through his grasp. Locking his arm around Grieco's chest and pinning his arms down, Crossfire raised his gun and started to walk toward the door. Pressing the gun into Grieco's temple, they burst through the door and into the night air.

"Show yourself, Latham!" Crossfire yelled as they made their way from the trailer.

"You won't live through this," Grieco sputtered.

"Quiet," Crossfire said calmly as he surveyed the area.

Hearing footsteps off to his right, Crossfire turned and saw two armed guards break off in different directions in an effort to surround him. Quickly moving the gun from Grieco's temple, he fired off a shot as one of the guards tried to take cover behind a cement truck. He watched as the henchman fell and landed just short of their destination. Turning the gun to the other guard, Crossfire swiftly opened fire.

The guard was making his way toward the limousine as the bullets tore through him. The man lurched forward and landed on the hood of Latham's vehicle before sliding lifelessly to the ground. Returning the pistol to Grieco's temple, Crossfire began to walk toward Latham.

"Come out of there, Latham! Show yourself, you coward!" Crossfire yelled as he pushed the gun hard into Grieco.

Focusing intently on the limousine, Crossfire failed to notice the nearby shadows come alive.

* * * * * *

The Wraith stepped out from the darkness and watched as Crossfire held Grieco for ransom in an attempt to coax Latham out of his car. Focusing intently on the job at hand, Crossfire was unable to see The Wraith approaching. He knew that if he attacked, Crossfire would certainly pull the trigger and eliminate Grieco where they stood. Attack, therefore, was not yet an option. However, The Wraith felt he could still end this situation before any more blood was shed.

"Let him go, Crossfire," The Wraith boomed as he edged in closer.

* * * * * *

Doesn't he ever quit?

Hearing the familiar voice of The Wraith was more than he needed at the moment. Turning to face the Dread Avenger, Crossfire decided to take what could well be his final stand.

Pushing Grieco face first into The Wraith, Crossfire turned and bolted toward the limousine. Running as fast as he could, he retrieved a hand grenade from his bag. Pulling the pin, he rolled the grenade under the vehicle and kept moving toward the framework of the looming structure.

* * * * * *

Latham saw the grenade fly from Crossfire's hand and quickly rolled out of the limousine.

"Get out of here!" he screamed as he motioned for his bodyguards to vacate the car.

They did so eagerly, leaping from the vehicle and running for their lives.

Scrambling away, Latham flopped onto the muddy ground and did his best to crawl away as fast as he could. Desperately trying to get to his feet, Latham stumbled before catching his footing and followed his bodyguards to take cover near a giant plow. Looking over, he saw Crossfire had vanished and The Wraith was helping Grieco back toward the leveled trailer.

As Latham glanced toward his vehicle, it suddenly erupted in a giant ball of flames, lifting off the ground from the force of the blast. The windows shattered and flew outward, covering the ground in a minefield of glass. It bounced as it came back to Earth, causing the front bumper to hang down and the rear door that had been left open from the escape to hang crookedly by a single bolt.

Anger welled up inside him. His plan to ambush Crossfire had backfired badly. The hunter had become the hunted, a situation that had become all too common in recent times. A situation he hated. Latham drew a small pistol from his muddied coat.

"Go get him," he said as he motioned in the direction Crossfire had headed. "And don't disappoint me. I want his head. His head, dammit!"

He watched as the three bodyguards cautiously raised their automatic rifles and crept toward the darkened building structure.

It's now or never, he thought.

He wasn't going to let some thug with a grudge take him out in the mud. Not this night.

* * * * * *

The Wraith sat Grieco up against the backside of the trailer and looked him over. The only wall of the trailer left standing made for decent cover under the circumstances.

"Can you stand?" The Wraith asked as he examined Grieco.

"Why did you save me?" Grieco asked, confusion in his eyes.

The Wraith didn't answer but instead peered around the corner of the trailer and checked the area. Having seen Crossfire take off into the shadows just before he leveled the limousine, The Wraith had to make sure no more lives were lost.

"If you're smart, you'll get your boss and yourself out of here," The Wraith said.

He watched for a response from Grieco but it never came. The man just stared at him blankly.

"Did you hear me?" The Wraith asked bluntly.

"I'm sure he did, Wraith," a familiar voice said from behind him.

Turning around, The Wraith came face to face with Robert Latham, who was pointing a gun directly at his head.

"Tonight, it looks like we're going to take care of two problems in one fell swoop," Latham said as a maniacal grin grew across his face.

* * * * * *

Crossfire watched from the shadows as the first guard stalked past him. Years of training and active service kicked in. He knew how to handle himself in situations such as these. As the first man walked directly by without seeing, Crossfire waited patiently for the next man.

When the second guard stepped within reach, Crossfire grabbed his weapon and aimed directly at the first guard. Pulling the trigger, he quickly gunned down the first guard before stripping the gun from the second. The moonlight eased through the clouds and shone down, illuminating the building site in a ghostly hue. Crossfire could see the fear on the second guard's face. Dropping the man's automatic rifle, he quickly threw his grip around his head and twisted. The sound of bones snapping in the man's neck indicated the battle, if one could call it that, was over.

Crossfire reached down, grabbed the rifle, slung it over his shoulder and trudged through the muddy area toward the trailers. The third guard appeared then and Crossfire dealt with him swiftly, plunging a knife into his chest in one deadly motion. It was over before it had a chance to begin.

* * * * * *

Latham nodded for Grieco to stand as he held his gun firmly at The Wraith's head. Watching his lieutenant struggle to his feet, Latham made sure Grieco had a firm footing before giving further direction.

"Let's both take out this menace together, Charlie," Latham said as he lowered his gun and aimed at The Wraith's chest.

As he did so, Grieco raised his own pistol and pressed it against The Wraith's head.

"If you kill me now," The Wraith said, holding his hands aloft, "you will almost certainly die at Crossfire's hands."

"He's right," a voice said from behind.

Turning his head slightly, Latham saw Crossfire standing directly behind him with an automatic rifle raised and ready to fire.

"I'm going to kill you right now," Crossfire continued.

Sizing up the situation, Latham felt his wildcard lay with Grieco. Shooting his deputy a glance and slightly twitching his eye, Latham dropped his pistol and raised his hands. Turning around, he saw the rifle barrel inches from his face.

"If you pull that trigger, you'll never find out exactly how your whole squad was set up," Latham said calmly as he watched the confusion dawn on Crossfire's face.

"What are you talking about?" Crossfire muttered quickly.

Latham watched Crossfire's finger twitch on the trigger. He knew the man couldn't resist hearing what he had to say.

"When you burst into my office, rambling nonsense about Iraq, I remembered something."

"Get on with it!" Crossfire spat.

"I have a colleague in the military. Pretty high up the ladder, actually. I asked him to hire someone, the best of the best, so to speak, to help retrieve the Monete Della Trinità. He suggested a private squad. Yours."

A momentary pause.

"I don't believe you," Crossfire said finally as he slightly lowered the rifle.

"Oh yes, it's true. I didn't know, or care, who he hired to do the job. I just needed some extra force in the area to assist my own private militia. With a second and more secretive group entering the area, I figured they might have had better luck than my people. With constant run-ins with the Iraqi military, it was becoming difficult to search that pitiful little village. I needed the best. I needed you."

"I'm going to make you suffer," Crossfire said after some moments of thought. "You'll beg me to end your life."

Crossfire stepped forward, dropped the rifle and raised his hands toward Latham's throat.

Seizing his opportunity, Latham fell to the ground. As he did so, he heard a gunshot echo through the construction site.

* * * * * *

Seeing Latham drop down was his cue. Peering from behind The Wraith, Grieco shakily shifted his pistol and fired. Crossfire's head snapped back and spurted blood high into the air. The villain fell backward and landed with a thud.

Focusing on Crossfire, Grieco turned his attention back to The Wraith just in time to see a gloved fist expand across his visual range. The impact sent him reeling backward and caused him to fall against part of the decimated trailer. Looking up, the darkened area seemed to grow even darker as he slipped away into unconsciousness.

* * * * * *

The Wraith quickly turned back and saw Crossfire lying in the mud a few yards away. The side of his head was bloody and it was beginning to pool beneath his head. He noticed Crossfire was barely breathing. It was faint enough that an untrained eye probably wouldn't be able to notice, but The Wraith saw. He wondered how Crossfire could have survived a shot to the head at point blank range.

As he stared at Crossfire's prone body, Latham began to stand and dusted himself off.

"Well, well, well. It looks like we did what you couldn't do, Wraith," Latham said with sadistic menace.

Eyeing his nemesis, The Wraith watched Latham survey the damage and enjoy his triumph. A moment later, Latham walked to where Crossfire lay and spat on his body.

"It's such a shame, really," Latham said as he turned his attention back to The Wraith. "He had potential."

With Crossfire still alive, The Wraith knew he had to do something or the villain would soon die.

* * * * * *

His head hurt and his body ached. He felt as if a train had hit him head on and he had lived to tell about it. He took in short, slow breaths and tried to remember what had just happened. Opening his eyes, he saw The Wraith and Latham through bleary eyes standing a few feet apart. Crossfire felt the blood run down the side of his face and instantly remembered he had been shot.

As he stared up at the two men, trying to think of a course of action, he caught a glimpse of The Wraith looking directly at him. The Wraith knew he wasn't dead.

Quickly grabbing the rifle lying beside him, Crossfire sat up and aimed it directly at Latham's back. Before he could squeeze the trigger, he saw The Wraith leap forward and shove Latham out of the way. The rifle fired, but the shot missed its target.

Standing up shakily, he saw The Wraith land directly in front of him.

* * * * * *

Stunned by Crossfire's quick recovery from a potentially mortal wound, The Wraith nevertheless sprung into action, kicking the rifle from Crossfire's grip. It landed out of sight with a metallic thud. Stepping in, he delivered two fast rights directly to Crossfire's jaw, causing the villain to stagger back. Crossfire rubbed at his face, smearing the blood around. He looked maniacal and The Wraith knew there was only one thing on his mind: death.

Readying himself, he saw Crossfire shake the punches off and charge at him. The impact was hard and took him completely backward. Landing in the mud, they rolled together furiously, Crossfire letting fly with a series of punches. The Wraith did his best to block them with his forearm wrist guards and waited for his next opportunity to strike.

Managing to twist his body and shake Crossfire off, The Wraith used his right arm to slam Crossfire face down in the mud. The Wraith then slung himself around and landed directly on Crossfire's back. Planting his knees deep in his lower back, The Wraith delivered several hard elbows to the side of Crossfire's head.

Crossfire planted his hands out in the mud, as if to push himself up, and flipped his body around, landing on his back. Surprised, The Wraith fell off and landed in a heap nearby. Before he could turn to face his enemy, Crossfire lashed out with a boot, connecting with The Wraith's jaw.

The pain was intense but he did his best to shake it off and focus. He would hurt when there was time. Rolling over onto his back, he saw Crossfire falling down on top of him. The Wraith grabbed Crossfire by the throat, tossed him off and staggered to his feet.

Crossfire landed near the building structure and disappeared into the darkness. As The Wraith moved to follow, Crossfire appeared from nowhere and slammed into him, causing him to bounce off a steel support beam. As soon as he hit the ground, Crossfire was on top of him again. He felt the strong grip reach around his neck and begin to tighten. Catching only glimpses of Crossfire's face as the clouds moved across the moon, The Wraith saw evil flash through the man's eyes.

Struggling to break Crossfire's grip, The Wraith heard footsteps closing in on them. He gripped Crossfire's wrists and twisted, causing the villain's grip to slacken slightly. Twisting and pulling further, The Wraith finally broke Crossfire's hold.

The light hit Crossfire again as the moon reappeared and The Wraith saw him draw a tiny blade from his belt.

"Goodbye, Wraith," Crossfire panted as he raised the knife to strike the killing blow.

Gunshots rang out. Crossfire was flung to one side while The Wraith rolled quickly into the darkness.

* * * * * *

"I hit him, sir," Grieco said as he lowered his gun. "I saw him fall. I don't understand how he survived."

Latham shot him an apprehensive look as they moved in close to the edge of the building frame. Looking around, Grieco saw only a darkened heap lying in the edge of the moonlight.

"There," he pointed.

Moving closer, he saw that The Wraith was gone and Crossfire lay motionless in the dirt. Latham turned to his deputy, anger written all over his face.

"Are you sure he's dead this time?" Latham asked with some menace.

Moving in closer, Grieco readied his pistol in case of attack. Cautiously extending his hand, he placed his fingers on Crossfire's neck. He couldn't detect a pulse.

"He's dead, sir. No doubt about it this time."

"Good," Latham said from behind him.

Grieco stood and walked back through the beams toward his boss, who waited on the edge of the building frame.

"Dispose of his body while I call for a pick up," Latham said as he walked toward the still-standing office trailer.

"What should I do with him?" Grieco asked.

"Cement him into the foundation," Latham said without stopping.

* * * * * *

The Wraith watched from the shadows as Grieco struggled to drag Crossfire to the edge of the building frame and rolled the lifeless body into a small ditch, which ran the length of the inside frame and stretched corner to corner. The Wraith saw the irony of Latham's new building being erected on the remains of one of his greatest enemies. If only he had been able to stop Crossfire in time, his death might have been prevented. He certainly could have been valuable in gathering evidence to bring down Latham once and for all. It wasn't to be, however.

Retreating through the shadows toward the waiting Daimler, The Wraith felt relief and a little sadness in knowing that the situation was finally over. Despite the atrocities Crossfire had committed, he knew Latham had been responsible, at least in part, for what Crossfire had become and he only hoped that, somehow, Captain Jackson Thomas was now at peace.

* * * * * *

The rumble of the cement truck echoed through the empty industrial park. The giant mixer coming to life created a rumble that reverberated through the truck and shook Grieco in the driver seat. As he backed the truck up to the building frame where Crossfire lay, he saw Latham inside the office trailer, sipping a cup of coffee and talking on his phone.

Grieco exited the truck. The clouds again moved, blocking the moon and sending the area into a blackened hue. Grieco walked to the back to drop the chute and fill the ditch with cement. Once there, he glanced in the ditch and couldn't believe his eyes. Even in the darkness he could see Crossfire's body was gone.

Panic set in as he ran around the truck, looking for the body. Drawing his pistol, he scanned the area for any sign of

Crossfire. The man had simply vanished, somehow escaping death once again.

No, wait a minute, Grieco thought. *The Wraith is still around here somewhere. He just stole the body. Yeah, that's it. No way could Crossfire still be alive. I checked his pulse myself.*

Heartened somewhat by his own spur of the moment solution, he made his way to the back of the truck and checked the ditch again. Crossfire was still nowhere to be seen. He craned his vision all around and saw movement in the shadows near the fence.

It must be The Wraith.

He held his gun aloft.

As the clouds parted, bathing the scene in a bright white light, he saw Crossfire standing on the fence line, staring back at him.

Frozen in place with fear, Grieco stared in disbelief as Crossfire merely stood there, staring right back at him. For what felt like an eternity, they continued thus before the clouds drifted lazily across the moon once again, engulfing Crossfire in the shadows.

Not knowing what to do, Grieco stood still. In the darkness, he saw what appeared to be Crossfire limping away deeper into the shadows. Picking up the courage to move, he raced forward, keeping his gun at the ready, and ran to the fence line. Once there, he was alone. Crossfire was gone. There was no sign of him anywhere and Grieco felt his heart jump into his throat. He couldn't let him get away but he couldn't report to Latham that Crossfire was still alive, either.

Running back to the truck, Grieco pulled the lever on the chute and began filling the ditch with cement. It slopped down thick and the smell of it drifted up through the air. Staring back at the fence, Grieco wondered if the battle was over, and if it wasn't, how long it would be before he saw Crossfire again.

The thoughts of letting Crossfire escape plagued him, but he ultimately decided that whatever Latham didn't know wouldn't hurt him.

Yet.

~ Epilogue ~

The sun shone brightly through the hospital room and woke Leena with the warm sensation of the dawn of a new day. Looking around her room, she saw the love of her life, Paul, sitting beside her and gazing out the window.

"Hey," she said sleepily.

"Good morning," Paul said, turning his attention from the window. "I've got great news. They're sending you home this afternoon."

"That's great," Leena said as she noticed a look of concern on his face. "How's Max?"

"He was beaten pretty badly," Paul revealed, "but he'll be just fine. A few bumps and bruises won't hold him down for long."

"Thank goodness," Leena said, relieved, though appalled at the punishment their close friend had endured. "And Crossfire?"

"Dead." Paul said solemnly.

"Dead? How?"

"Grieco," Paul returned. "I'll fill you in on everything once I get you home, okay?"

"Sure," Leena said as she took his hand and squeezed tightly. She noticed him wince as she grabbed his hand. "I'm glad it's over."

"Me too," Paul said. "Me too."

* * * * * *

Sitting at her desk, Detective Perez glanced at the empty work desk beside hers and couldn't help but miss her partner. After spending all night in the hospital, making sure Sloan was okay and his wife had company, she was relieved to come back to work and decompress.

Looking over the stack of memos and papers that littered her desk, she saw an envelope addressed to her lying on the top. She opened it up and saw it was short and directly to the point:

Detective Perez,
The menace has been eliminated by a third party.
-W

Knowing what—or who—the W stood for, she immediately shoved the letter and envelope into the paper shredder that rested on top of her waste basket. Her mind raced with the possibilities of who the third party was, but the only one that made sense to her was Robert Latham. She wondered just what had happened.

As she thought, Commissioner Harrison walked up and startled her with his presence.

"You're gonna have to drag Sloan out of that hospital bed," he said smiling. "I need my two best detectives on this."

He handed her a manila folder.

"Sir, what is this about?" Perez asked.

"After you left the warehouse that exploded last night at the harbor, rescue teams found a man's body that had washed up nearby. We don't think it was related to the explosion, as investigators just told me they believe the body was killed at a different location and dumped in the water," Harrison related. "Body parts missing. Nasty piece of work."

"I'll get on it right away, sir," Perez said as she tried to push Crossfire and The Wraith from her mind.

"Oh, and Perez, this is the second such killing this week," Harrison said before turning and walking away.

Opening the folder, Perez spread it out on top of the stack that covered her desk. Grabbing the papers inside, she sat back and started to read.

* * * * * *

Latham sat in his high-back leather office chair, reading the newspaper. Hearing footsteps, he casually looked up to see Grieco limping across his office.

"Is the site clean, Charlie?" Latham probed.

"Yes, sir. I called some extra help in after you left last night. I just came from there. The site is clean. No evidence of anything untoward happening there."

Grieco slid into the chair across from Latham.

"Then no one will ever know I've built part of my empire on Crossfire," Latham said with a wink.

"No, sir," Grieco replied. "No one will ever know."

* * * * * *

The sun beat down and cooked the back of his neck. It had been a long time since he had been in this area. As he stepped through the thick sand and made his way up a tiny hill, he could see the village below.

Not much further now.

Crossfire trudged across the valley toward Karbah and cursed the heat. He had spent so long in Metro City, where the climate was quite moderate, that he had forgotten how unforgiving the Iraqi sun could be.

As he reached the main road leading into Karbah, he saw a small crowd of men rush from the village to block his path. He stopped dead in his tracks, holding up his hands in surrender. The men, all brandishing weapons ranging from knives and rocks to assault rifles, circled him and closed him off from the village.

After a brief moment, the crowd split and an elderly man made his way past the men toward Crossfire. Stopping just short of him, Crossfire recognized the man and nodded. Returning the nod, the man smiled at Crossfire and extended his hand.

Crossfire slowly lowered his right hand and carefully placed it in his pocket. He pulled his hand out and turned it over to reveal a golden coin. The older man took the coin and studied it closely. After a moment spent studying the specimen, the man smiled and motioned for Crossfire to follow him.

"Thank you for lending me the coin. My mission failed, but it aided in my survival," Crossfire said as he walked along beside the man. "The legend was true."

Stopping, the man looked up at him and gave an understanding nod. Crossfire returned the motion as the man reached up and placed a bony hand on his shoulder.

"Will you be staying with us long?" the man asked in a thick accent.

"Indefinitely," Crossfire said.

"Good. I am overjoyed to see you return."

"Funnily enough...so am I," Crossfire said.

It was true. Despite the heat and the terrible things that happened to him in this village, in this country, Crossfire felt strangely at peace in Karbah. It had somehow become the closest thing to a home to him. Perhaps it was the people there. Perhaps it was because this was where he last served with his close comrades and felt their presence there more than anywhere else. He didn't know for sure, he only knew the way he felt.

The man motioned for Crossfire to follow and they parted the crowd in front of them. Walking toward the village, and seeing the people cheering and smiling at his presence, Crossfire felt alive for the first time in a long time.

He needed to be here, needed time to think, to regroup. To relax. He realized his mission to Metro City had been a failure and that realization irked him beyond measure.

Next time will be different though, he thought.

And there would be a next time, rest assured of that. Only the next time he would be waging a war on two fronts...one against Robert Latham and another against The Wraith.

And this time he would win.

~ Author's Note ~

I'm so happy to get this new edition finally into print, featuring its new Glowing Eyes Media trade dress, and reflecting the correct authorship of this story. While the original plot and first draft came from my good friend and colleague, Stephen J. Semones, I honed the story into what you are now reading, so the updated credits now properly reflect this. I hope you enjoyed reading *Crossfire*.

As Stephen has now pretty much retired frm writing (opting to focus more on his new career as a pastor, along with his third wife, Faith), it's up to me to provide this updated Author's Note for this new edition.

Stephen's initial story was an excellent one, and I was more than eager to add it to the burgeoning collection in *The Wraith Dread Avenger of the Underworld* series. His villain character, Crossfire, fuelled my imagination, so much so I used him again in a later Wraith novel, *Vendetta* (and I have plans for his future return). So, the ultimate thanks must go to Stephen, for crafting such an amazing story, and for creating such an amazing villain. His friendship and support over the years was greatly valued. I feel his loss to the writing world immensely, but it is, of course, up to him how he lives his life. How he achieves fulfillment and joy is always his own decision, and I wish him the very best in the future. God bless, my friend.

Secondly, I want to thank my family, my wife, Jennifer, my daughter, Emma and my mum and sister. They have always been there for me and always will be. Your love and support means the world to me. Thank you from the bottom of my heart. Thank you also to my editor, Joanne Lane, from FirstEditing.com, for such a fine job in honing this tome.

And, last but by no means least, to all my fans and readers. What I do I ultimately do for you. All these books are for you. And there will be many more to come, I can assure you. Without you and your support, these books wouldn't happen. So thank you, one and all.

This story sprang from Stephen's furtive imagination, his desire to tell an action thriller with links to the military, while also incorporating. Initially intended as a four-part comic book mini-series, it was retooled as a novel after Glowing Eyes Media (then Trinity Comics) segued away from comics and into the prose arena. Stephen initially had some trouble focusing on the story at hand, but with support and prodding from his then (second) wife, Autumn, and myself, he finally got the story going, and it then began to flow well.

You will see some initial cover ideas in the subsequent pages, from the Bridgeforth Design Studio and, if you are interested in the further adventures of The Wraith, please read on for a look at all the books now available, either direct from Glowing Eyes Media, or through your favorite book stockists. Thank you.

All the best
Frank Dirscherl
Wollongong NSW, 2025

Original cover sketch by Brian Bridgeforth

Finished cover sketch by Brian Bridgeforth

Wraith sketch by Brian Bridgeforth

CULT OF THE DAMNED

~ Sneak peek ~

Here is a special sneak peek at the following novel, #3 in
the series, *Cult of the Damned*. Please enjoy chapter 1 of this
exciting book...

~ Prologue ~

The rain pummeled down from the night sky in sheets as thick as lead. The furious onslaught from the heavens lashed the windshield of the armored truck as it rumbled down the busy Metro City thoroughfare. Life never took a breather in a city like Metro, and even at 4 A.M. in such inclement weather, the streets were teeming with people and cars of all descriptions. Car horns blared, certain people—johns, hookers, bums, cops—mill about, yelling, weeping, running, fighting. Night was always a bleak time in Metro City, and this night was no exception.

"Man, what a time to be delivering this cargo," Ralph said from the passenger seat of the armored truck. "Why the heck do we get stuck with all the crap jobs, Jim?" Ralph was a burly, heavy-set man in his fifties with a full, graying mustache and heavily-lidded eyes. He shifted uncomfortably in his seat, while his partner peered intently through the windshield, trying to keep control of the truck in the appalling conditions.

Jim shrugged his shoulders. "And why do we have to deliver this thing at this ungodly hour?"

"Because Mr. Latham told us to," said Ralph, who noted Jim's sour expression. He sighed. "Mr. Latham thought it best to deliver such valuable cargo at a time when there was the least chance of anything going wrong. That work better for you?"

Jim, younger, slimmer and less hairy than his co-pilot, arched an eyebrow. "Yeah, but that doesn't reflect well on us though, does it? I can't wait to get rid of it. Darn thing gives me the creeps."

"Ah well. Latham pays for the service, so who are we to argue?"

"What is it exactly anyway?" Jim queried. "Some voodoo piece?"

"I don't know, and I don't really care. All I know is we were warned it shouldn't be touched under any circumstances. Something about it being dangerous. Beats me how, though."

Jim shivered at the mention of the word *dangerous*.

The truck inched its way through the torrential rain, down the hectic Montgomery Street, swarming as it was with that particular brand of nightlife for which Metro had long since become infamous. Red light turning green, Jim veered into the narrower Harris Street, and then out into the wider expanse of Joseph Boulevard.

"Are you sure we're going the right way?" Jim asked, guiding the truck as best he could down the wide, lengthy road. He fiddled with the de-frost controls on the truck's dashboard, trying to get it working but without much luck. The windshield was fogged over.

"Yeah, yeah, turn here," Ralph replied. He removed a handkerchief from his right-side trouser pocket, and wiped the windshield clear as best he could.

Jim moved the truck onto George Avenue and finally toward the looming Metro City Gallery. The lights of the gallery shone through the foggy windshield in bright blotches as the truck turned and drove carefully up the short drive, coming to a halt at a security gate.

Jim wound down his window. "Hey, where do we deliver this?" he asked the guard in the small booth beside them.

"You the special delivery guys?" the guard shouted above the din of the pouring rain. Jim nodded. "Go round the turn there and then head to the back." The guard thumbed to somewhere further down the drive.

"Yeah, okay. Sure thing," Jim said and rolled up the window. "I'll be glad to hand this stuff over and get back home. I can just catch a few hours sleep before my next shift. I hate night shifts." He drove the truck further down the drive as directed.

"Especially in this kind of weather," Ralph said. "You think it's ever going to stop raining? How long's it been, two weeks? I'm practically growing gills already."

"I read in the paper it's expected to rain most of this month. Climate change they call it," Jim said, as he parked the truck in the circular loading zone protected from the elements by a large overhead awning. "C'mon, let's get this over with."

The two security officers exited the truck and moved back to the vehicle's rear door, the sound of their footsteps barely distinguishable from that of the rain. They looked up to see a tall, well-dressed man with thinning hair and a grin that would make the Cheshire Cat green with envy approaching them from the gallery's loading dock. He was flanked by several uniformed armed guards, ready to take possession of the truck's goods.

"Gentlemen, my name is Bartholomew Gregory. I'm the curator of this gallery," greeted the curator in a hearty tone. "I am so glad to see you've arrived with our invaluable artifact."

"What is this we're hauling, exactly? Some voodoo stone or something?" Jim asked while opening the truck's rear door.

"An artefact that is absolutely priceless," Gregory said, still smiling. "The Cortes Stone, an ancient Aztec stone carving, depicting one of their gods, Huitzilopochtli, defeating the invading Spaniards led by Hernando Cortes. It was only recently discovered in the wilds of Mexico in a heretofore undiscovered tomb. Our great patron, Robert Latham ensured this international treasure would make its home here as part of this city's two-hundredth anniversary celebration."

Ralph looked to Jim and rolled his eyes. Jim knew what he meant. *Is this guy reading off a cue card?*

"Well, here's your precious carving, packed away nice and tight," Ralph said, indicating inside the truck.

"I cannot thank you enough for your vigilance and speedy arrival here. I shall make sure Mr. Latham hears of your exemplary work," Gregory said. The curator indicated his own guards to take charge of the situation, which they promptly did, surrounding the truck carefully, their guns raised in readiness for any eventuality. From the rear of the loading dock several workmen appeared, dressed in overalls, one of whom pulled a metallic trolley behind him.

"Uh, yeah, well, thanks," Ralph said, scratching his head with the one hand while brandishing a clipboard with the other. "Now, if you could just sign here, Mr.—"

"Over there, please be careful with the package," Gregory shouted to one of the workmen, ignoring Ralph. "It's your jobs if you drop it."

Two of the workmen climbed into the truck and removed the fastenings securing the wooden crate to the truck floor. They then carefully shifted the large crate to the edge of the truck, then onto the awaiting trolley.

"Now, let's get this inside and away from this atrocious weather," Gregory said, turning on his heels and quickly making his way back into the gallery. The workmen, with the secured carving, followed suit, the gallery's security guards remaining on alert.

"Uh...Mr. Gregory?" Ralph shouted, waving his clipboard. "Could you—" But Gregory had already disappeared, vanishing within the bowels of the city gallery. Ralph looked to Jim, who merely shrugged his shoulders. "C'mon, we have to get this guy's signature before we can leave."

They strode the path down into the loading dock and climbed the stairs up into the main loading area. They were greeted by a plethora of crates and boxes of all sizes and lighting so low as to be almost sinister, the boxes and crates casting eerie shadows on the walls surrounding them.

"Where'd they get to?" Jim asked, stumbling around in the darkness.

"Over there." Ralph pointed. "There's some light."

The two arrived at a partially-open wooden door. A weak light shone from the other side. Peering round, Jim saw a long, narrow corridor snaking down toward a murky center.

"Take a look," Jim said and let Ralph grab a peek.

"I guess they went that way," Ralph said, again scratching his head.

They passed through the corridor, entered the larger, darkened room beyond, then heard voices coming from yet another room, the entrance to which lay ahead of them.

"This way. Let's just get this signed so we can get outta this maze," Ralph muttered.

They passed through this last doorway to find themselves in a large, cavernous area with high glass ceilings and low, moody lighting. The rain beat down on the glass, its steady drum rumbling throughout the room. Paintings and etchings of incredible beauty and intricacy lined the walls. Bartholomew Gregory and three of his workmen stood at the far side of the room. The armed guards were nowhere in sight.

"Careful. The stone is the most precious piece we've ever received," Gregory said.

As the two security officers walked over to join him, two of the three workmen cautiously pried open the wooden crate containing the carving.

"Mr. Gregory, we need your—" Ralph started to say but was cut off by a wave of the hand.

"Hmm...? Oh, yes, one moment please," the curator replied absently.

With the wooden crate open, a gloved workman lifted a small, rounded, stone slab roughly twelve inches in diameter above the rim of the crate. Gregory's eyes shone bright at the sight of it. The surface of the stone was decorated with carvings of unique and complex beauty, with depictions of various figures that neither Jim nor Ralph recognized.

"It's even more beautiful than I could have ever imagined," Gregory said under his breath. "See the great sun god wreaking vengeance on the Conquistadors? And here," he indicated to one of the figures on the carving, "on Cortes himself. A depiction of the Aztec Indians greatest desire, and one which they sadly never realized." He stopped to catch his breath. "And the jade embossing the rim...it is an amazing piece." Gregory straightened. "Put it over there." And nodded toward the stand, shaped much like a speaker's lectern, nearby.

The workman holding the stone laid it gently into its ready-made cradle at the top of the stand.

"Good," Gregory said, still marveling over the stone. "I find I cannot take my eyes off this. It's as though I..."

He moved closer to the object. "I need to—" He reached out to touch the carving, to run his fingers along its elaborate imagery of godly vengeance.

"Mr. Gregory, no!" Ralph cried.

But it was too late.

Gregory's face lit up in apparent ecstasy as he felt the texture of the stone and its carvings, then lurched backward, coughing, his body heaving violently. He collapsed in a heap on the gallery floor—and quickly disintegrated into ash before the shocked eyes of those present.

~ Also Available ~

THE WRAITH

The Wraith Dread Avenger of the Underworld #1
THE WRAITH
Frank Dirscherl

In a world not far removed from our own, a city lies ravaged. Crime overruns its streets, its citizens are helpless. Crime lord Robert Latham holds the city in his sway. One man, however, stands above the rest, willing to fight for freedom. That man is The Wraith!

NOW AVAILABLE!

www.glowingeyesmedia.com

The Wraith Dread Avenger of the Underworld #2
VALLEY OF EVIL
Frank Dirscherl

After the horror the Cobra unleashed upon Metro City, Paul Sanderson has recuperated, regained his strength and focus, and the city has been rebuilt while its citizens have slowly started to regroup and move forward. Into this relative calm marches Ma Tzi, the Hong Kong drug lord, who senses a weakness in resident crime lord Robert Latham's hold on the city and intends to exploit that in any way necessary. And at any cost.

NOW AVAILABLE!

www.glowingeyesmedia.com

The Wraith Dread Avenger of the Underworld #6

SWAMP WITCH OF SATAN'S FOREST

Frank Dirscherl & Ray MacKay

On their way home from their mountain vacation which was anything but, Paul Sanderson (aka The Wraith) and his love Leena Patterson are waylaid by a mysterious cry for help, and are unwittingly drawn into the forest—and the web—of the alluring Swamp Witch.

NOW AVAILABLE!

www.glowingeyesmedia.com

The Wraith Dread Avenger of the Underworld #7
VENDETTA
Frank Dirscherl

Having gone through ordeal after ordeal, Paul Sanderson (aka The Wraith Dread Avenger of the Underworld ®) and his love Leena Patterson, decide to take a long overdue vacation. However, their idyll is soon shattered by an attack by a creature nobody thought could possibly exist—a werewolf. Soon, an evil so heinous makes himself known, and only The Wraith could possibly defeat it.

NOW AVAILABLE!

www.glowingeyesmedia.com

The Wraith Dread Avenger of the Underworld #8
LADY WRAITH
Frank Dirscherl & Adam Oravec

The Wraith is missing. No one has seen him since going out on patrol. Now, the love of his life Leena Patterson, must sally forth on her own as Lady Wraith, protect the city, find her love, and combat a deadly new adversary hell-bent on destruction, while also dealing with rampant police corruption and sex slavery.

COMING SOON!

www.glowingeyesmedia.com

Books of Judgment Book Two
SERPENT RISING
Frank Dirscherl & Greg Gick

Having gone through ordeal after ordeal, Paul Sanderson (aka The Wraith Dread Avenger of the Underworld ®) and his love Leena Patterson, decide to take a long overdue vacation. However, their idyll is soon shattered by an attack by a creature nobody thought could possibly exist—a werewolf. Soon, an evil so heinous makes himself known, and only The Wraith could possibly defeat it.

NOW AVAILABLE!

www.glowingeyesmedia.com

About the Type

Garamond is a group of many old-style serif typefaces, originally those designed by Parisian craftsman Claude Garamond and other 16th century French engravers, and now many modern revivals. Though his name was written as 'Garamont' in his lifetime, the typefaces are generally spelled 'Garamond'. **Garamond Normal**, used in this book, is one of those modern revivals.

Join FRANK DIRSCHERL and Glowing
Eyes Media on social media!

facebook.com/glowingeyesmedia

@glowingeyesmedia

instagram.com/glowingeyesmedia

glowingeyesmedia.proboards.com

All Glowing Eyes Media, The Wraith and Starflame
novels, comics and merchandise can be obtained
directly from the Glowing Eyes Media website –
www.glowingeyesmedia.com

Want to be The Wraith?

Well, it might be hard to actually *be* The Wraith, unless of course you, too, have been endowed with the power of the Eyes of Judgment. But you can certainly dress, drink and drive like him [*] (and you don't always have to be a millionaire to do so). See for yourselves.

The Wraith/Paul Sanderson wears:

- tailored clothing from Cad & the Dandy Tailors and Shirtmakers – www.cadandthedandy.co.uk
- bespoke footwear from Gaziano & Girling – www.gazianogirling.com
- watches from Héron (Marinor in Atlantic Blue) -

www.heronwatches.com/collections/marinor/products/marinor-atlantic-blue
- Armani Code cologne from Giorgio Armani – www.giorgioarmanibeauty-usa.com/for-him-armani-code/for-him-armani-code,default,sc.html

drinks:

- Twinings Earl & Lady Grey tea – www.twinings.co.uk
- Vittoria coffee – www.vittoriacoffee.com/

---

[*] Please note: Glowing Eyes Media does not condone drinking and driving. **All** adults, please always drink responsibly and **never** drink and drive

- The Balvenie Scotch whisky – www.thebalvenie.com
- Armand de Brignac champagne – www.armanddebrignac.com
- Cosmopolitan cocktails

uses:

- Dell laptops – www.dell.com.au
- Chesterfield furniture from Abbey Furniture www.chesterfieldfurnituremelbourne.com.au
- wallets from Launer - www.launer.com
- a Samsung Galaxy J5 Pro cell phone - www.samsung.com/latin_en/smartphones/galaxy-j5-2017/SM-J530GZDITPA/

drives:

- a Rolls Royce Wraith – www.rolls-roycemotorcars.com/en-GB/wraith.html

And, if you're really eager to actually look like The Wraith—in full costume—then you can always head over to Xtreme Design FX and let Lance Coulter there make you an exact replica of the costume used for The Wraith motion picture - www.xtremedesignfx.com